The Seven Princesses:
Quest to Arcadia

The Seven Princesses: Quest to Arcadia

Elizabeth Hunt

Believer's Dream Publishing

All Rights Reserved. Published in the United States by Believer's Dream Publishing.

www.believersdreampublishing.com

The text of this book is set in 12-point Calisto Mt. Printed in the United States of America

ISBN: 978-0-557-36934-8

Second edition

First printing, December 2010

Table of Contents:

Ripped from a perfect world before their birth
At age sixteen with midnight powers come
A brutal fight for everything they're worth
They must win or else Faerie will succumb
To evil, murky darkness, and despair
The monsters rising up at the New Year
Will challenge faeries every single heir
Against such vicious foes triumphs unclear
Yet an old prophecy foretells their win
Seven girls who will bring peace to us all
Every monster is paying for their sin
In the deep, dank, dark pit of their downfall
The seven princesses' together reign
And in their faerie kingdom shall remain

Chapter 1

_____ Getting Gowns_____

'Tania awoke to the pounding of her sister's fists upon her door. She knew why they were there; today was the day of their birthday party. 'Tania hated large gatherings like this, but the rest of her siblings loved them. 'Tania dragged herself out of her oak bed with its sky blue sheets and quilt and pulled on a pair of jeans and a t-shirt. Only then did she succumb to the wrath of her six sisters.

"'Tania, come on, you know we have to go down to the costume shop to get our regal clothes!" Demy exclaimed, trying not to show her enthusiasm as she jumped onto the bed and sat down. It wasn't working for her.

"I can't wait to see what my dress looks like!" Milæyka excitedly babbled. "The house is perfect for a royal ball." All seven sisters were going as princesses of the royal family. The house looked like a castle already, with large stonewalls and a vaguely medieval interior.

"You've said that seven times already, Milæyka." Selena teased lightly. 'Tania smiled as the rest of her sisters joined in the teasing. It was so hard to stay annoyed at

3

them for long. It wasn't often they could lift all the worries that came with being a high school student off of their shoulders and just have fun and act like little kids.

"Okay! I'm ready," 'Tania yelled as she finished brushing her long blonde hair. "Let's go before Mom gives up on us." The sisters laughed and headed out the door.

"I can't wait for the party! We have to be the only girls in all of Pacific Heights who have never had a big party before," Milæyka said (again) as they were heading down the curving stone staircase with its red velvet carpet.

Their mother had been the second known person to have a living set of septuplets. The public had scorned her at first because she had had no family and no memory of how she had conceived the children. Emma, their mom, had been hit by a car and went into labor. The combined stress of the car hit and the birth had given Emma amnesia. When they had tried to trace Emma's DNA they couldn't match it to anybody. After that, the hospital had tested for drugs and alcohol abuse. Neither were positive. Since they couldn't prove Emma would be a bad mother, the hospital had allowed her to keep the babies.

People had raised money to build a house big enough for the family, and volunteers helped take care of the seven babies. Emma had started her life anew after her daughters were born. She went to school for four years to qualify for a job, while she left her daughters at a daycare nearby. The money the people raised kept coming until the girls were seven, old enough to take care of themselves if their mother was busy. By then Emma had finished her four-year college program and had found a job working with a professor to teach medieval lifestyles to college kids. The seven girls also learned the medieval lifestyles, which led to their interest in princesses, dragons, and everything fantastical.

"Come on guys, we're going to be late!" Emma called.

"Coming, Mom," Bella shouted down the remainder of the stairs. The seven sisters ran down the rest of the stairs and hurried into the van.

❈ ❈ ❈ ❈ ❈

"Welcome to Costume Emporium- the number one place to buy costumes for any occasion," greeted the desk clerk.

"Hello. We are here to pick up eight royal family costumes," Emma told the clerk.

"Name?" the clerk asked.

"The costumes should be under Pleiades," Emma stated. The hospital had assigned a last name to the family due to the fact that Emma couldn't remember hers. They had decided to name the family after the constellation Pleiades, also known as the "Seven Sisters." Humorous but annoying, and the girls had always been made fun of for their last name.

The clerk came back with eight wonderfully made dresses that would have looked perfect in any movie. They were made the exact same way, but with changes in color and accessories. The girls oohed and aahed at the silky material that made up the slashes in the skirt and arms and the velour skirts that most of the dress was made of.

The dresses were unbelievably wonderful. "I never thought they would be this beautiful!" exclaimed Autumn.

"They will make us look perfect tonight, just like real princesses," Selena said in awe. She picked up her dress. It had a midnight blue skirt and top with peach slashes in panels down the skirt and on the top. Draping it over her arm, she caressed the fabric. Everyone, even 'Tania, knew that they were going to have fun tonight.

❈ ❈ ❈ ❈ ❈

"What is that?" Demy asked as she came in the door to find streamers and balloons strewn across the floor.

"Sorry about this, miss. We had a piñata that would break open at midnight and let loose golden chocolate coins, steamers and balloons filled with helium so they wouldn't fall, just float," said the befuddled decorator, a foreign lady with a short bob cut and painted jeans.

"So... what went wrong?" Milæyka asked in confusion.

"The *idiots* that work for me brought the wrong piñata! I sent them back to get the correct one while I cleaned up this mess." The decorator looked seriously frazzled.

"Here, we'll put our dresses in our rooms then we can come and help you," Bella said kindly as she helped the decorator to her feet. The seven sisters hurried up the stairs and hung their dresses up so they could help their mother with cooking and the decorator with her mess.

'Tania looked in the mirror before going back downstairs. She looked so young, much younger than her six other sisters. Even Autumn and Bella didn't look quite so young. One of their teachers used to say, "Everyone grows old, but only some people grow up." They all knew that 'Tania was the only one who never quite grew up in spirit. 'Tania quickly stopped her train of thought, for she knew that at the right times she could act older than her sisters by years, or have fun like she was a little kid. She thought of the mess downstairs and Bella's offer to help clean it up. That was just like her—always being kind and helpful.

'Tania didn't mind, but sometimes Bella's offers got the sisters into all sorts of unpleasant situations. Like when they had to house most of the town because their houses had been blown down or damaged by an earthquake. 'Tania quickly looked at her clock and ran back downstairs. There were seven hours until the party that were going to be busy for all of them.

Chapter 2

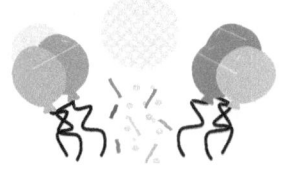

_____ Party_____

The seven sisters looked in the full-length mirror taking up one of the walls in the little antechamber at the top of the grand staircase, waiting for the announcement to come downstairs. One at a time, in order of birth, the girls would be called downstairs by their full names and would line up at the bottom. Seven boys would be waiting to come forward and dance with the seven "princesses." Since they were dressed as princesses, the party was going to feel like a royal ball. At midnight, the girls would cut the cake, exactly when they turned 16. It was 11 o'clock now. As they looked in the mirror, each girl felt confident and excited as well as nervous. Everyone would be watching them dance.

"Girls, line up—it's starting." Their Mom came in and gave them each a reassuring hug. "It'll be fun, just you wait."

"Introducing the seven princesses of the evening. Milæyka Reye Pleiades." Emma gave Milæyka a gentle shove toward the grand staircase and smiled.

"I'll go around back and watch you dance," their mother said as she turned to go. "Make sure you walk slowly and carefully with your head up and back straight. I'm so proud of you guys." As she left, Milæyka stepped out of the door and down the stairs.

"Selena Mirë Pleiades." Selena smiled and followed Milæyka down the staircase.

"Demeter Dove Pleiades, Titania Anne Pleiades, December Eve Pleiades, Autumn Rush Pleiades, and Bella Talih Pleiades." The announcer read all the girls names off.

'Tania walked down the long red-velvet carpeted staircase leading down to the ballroom. Looking up at her from the floor were people from school, around the neighborhood, and from her mother's school.

"Boys, please come forward." The announcer said.

'Tania rolled her eyes as Jake walked forward and took her hand. He had black hair and light blue eyes and was a little bit taller than her. She could see why Selena liked him. He was slightly tanned and his blue eyes made him look like a movie star, especially when he was wearing his black tux. She took his hand and walked forward onto the dance floor as a waltz started playing in the background. She knew she should say something, but she couldn't think of what. After all, he was her sister's boyfriend. "Ummm, how do like the party?"

"It's okay, but I uh, have to tell you guys something… I know your father." Jake blurted out the last part as fast as he could then steeled himself in case she hit him. He hadn't meant to say it then, especially when 'Tania was being nice to him, as she rarely was.

"My father?" 'Tania didn't know what to think. Her mom knew nothing of their father; how could this boy know something their mother didn't?

"Yes, he sent me here to find you and your family so

8

he could be reunited with you," Jake said apologetically.

"How come he hasn't tried to find us before now? Why did he send *you*? Why did you play with my sister's heart? Why did you pretend to love her?" 'Tania asked each question getting angrier all the time, her teeth grinding every time. She took a step forward with every word and Jake backed up.

Selena was her favorite sister, and this boy had pretended to love her just to get close to the family! 'Tania's temper had always been thin around Jake because of his smirky attitude, though when 'Tania thought about it, Selena had the exact same attitude and always had. For some reason it just bugged her in Jake.

"He only just found where you were, and I didn't pretend to love Selena. Well, maybe at first, but not now." Jake realized he should have played his cards differently in this conversation. If only he had been assigned to one of the other girls, maybe they would have been more ready to believe him. 'Tania had never liked him, and she had shut herself in a mental box as soon as he had mentioned her father.

"Why isn't he here himself?" 'Tania wanted to punch Jake, but what if he was telling the truth? For so long she had wanted a father to play with and hug. Could he have the ticket she needed?

"He wanted to be here, but he thought your mother might report him to the police if she didn't recognize him." Jake wasn't sure if 'Tania would believe him, but luckily she never had the chance to reply.

"Switch partners." the announcer came on the speakers and signaled the start of another dance. As Jake left to dance with Demy, another boy took 'Tania's hand and started spinning her around to the ballroom music that was playing.

"Demy, would you believe me if I told you I could

take you somewhere you could never imagine?" Jake had decided to approach the topic from a different angle.

"Maybe. Where is this place? Would Selena be going with you?" Demy was surprised that Jake sounded like he was hitting on her. From the look 'Tania had given him she didn't think his conversation with her had been very nice either. She guessed he had gone through this same routine with her and she had freaked out. As she always did when boys asked her questions that might lead to dates. Especially if the guy asking already had a girlfriend. If he said he wasn't taking Selena, Demy was going to smack him so hard....

"I was going to take your whole family to the place, then show you guys a secret I figured out." Jake realized that his first comment had been too forward. The last thing he needed was for her to think he was cheating on Selena.

Demy visibly relaxed when what Jake said proved he wasn't cheating on Selena. "Where would this place be that we couldn't imagine?" Demy was interested in this supposed place that would attract her whole family. That was a hard feat not many places could manage.

"It is a wonderful place. It is almost like a secret world." Jake decided not to mention he was born there, in case she thought it was a hospital. (That was what his teacher said humans were born in.)

"And when would you take us?" Demy questioned with a smile.

"How about after the party?" Jake asked.

"Won't it be awfully late?" Demy broke Jake's trance. "Most normal places will be closed by the time the party ends."

"It doesn't matter what time it is where I come from."

"Where do you come from?" Demy wondered where in the world nobody cared what time it was. Perhaps they didn't have clocks and that was why...

"I'm from... Alaska." Jake said the first state that popped into his mind.

"Really? Don't they have like six months of darkness at a time?" Demy asked.

"Something like that," Jake replied, a little confused. He had no idea what she was talking about since he wasn't from Earth, and hadn't really studied it.

"Switch partners!" Jake sighed with relief as he left Demy to find the girl he knew he could get to believe him—Selena.

Selena looked around and giggled when she saw Jake coming towards her.

"Be careful with Jake—he's been acting odd tonight," 'Tania said as she walked past Selena.

"How so?" Selena wondered, turning around slightly to follow 'Tania with her eyes as she walked by.

"He claims he knows our father, and I heard him telling Demy he was from Alaska." 'Tania's eyes were full of misgivings.

Jake finished his walk to Selena and without a single glance at 'Tania asked Selena to dance.

"I'd love to dance," Selena said as Jake twirled her off to the dance floor. "'Tania says you know our father," she said as a conversation opener.

"Umm... I know him and he has asked me to take you to him... 'Tania didn't think I was telling the truth, but I am." He was beginning to sound desperate. "The reason he couldn't find you was because he and your mother and you guys are fairies and he's stuck in the Kingdom of Faerie." Jake cursed himself for not getting to Selena before 'Tania.

"'Tania was right, you are acting weird." Selena laughed as Jake twirled her around again.

"It's true—you're a fairy! Your father sent me to you so I could convince you and your family to go through the

11

portal to the kingdom," Jake blurted out perhaps a little loudly.

"So you never loved me?" Selena asked as she stopped dancing and stepped away from Jake, her eyes betraying the confusion and hurt she felt.

"No, I mean yes... I mean, I asked you out the first time as a pretense, yes, but after that I really did fall in love with you. Believe me, Selena."

"How can I? How can I believe you? You say I'm a fairy, but I have no wings or special powers!"

"The type of fairy I'm talking about doesn't have wings, and... you are special," Jake said with a soft look in his eyes. "You will become more special tonight when the wind blows through your hair."

Selena looked back into Jake's eyes and saw her reflection staring back at her. With that look Selena knew that Jake genuinely thought that she was a fairy. What did that mean? Was he insane? Selena's eyes filled with tears as she realized how much it hurt to think that he had never loved her. She pushed away his hand on hers and turned around to leave.

"Selena... there's one more thing." Jake waited until she turned around to continue. "My real name is Caleb."

Selena turned and fast-walked to the punch table trying to hold back the tears. She couldn't believe that Jake/Caleb had lied to her for two whole months.

"Hey Selena," Milæyka said as she grabbed some punch.

"Uh, hi Milæyka," Selena said as she wiped her eyes and turned to face her.

"We are going to cut the cake soon," Milæyka said as she studied Selena's face wondering at the brimming tears. "Come on."

"Hello, your majesty," Caleb said as Emma walked by, her dress was similar to the princesses' dresses, but it had more layers and was cream and white.

"Why hello Jake, do you know where my daughters are?" Emma asked, completely unaware of Jake's issue with Selena.

"Yes, I believe I heard Milæyka say something about getting all the princesses to meet up with you at the bottom of the dais." Caleb wanted to tell the queen about her husband, Thíshién, but if she had no memory…

"Thank you Jake,"

As Emma left, Caleb used his last hope, her real name. "Goodbye, Queen Emmaralda."

"What did you call me?" Emma asked, in a hushed tone, half turned around.

"Emmaralda…your name." Caleb could see the queen's eyes start to recognize the name.

"Mom, come on." Bella said as the seven sisters walked by. Selena wouldn't meet Caleb's eyes.

With one last look at Caleb, Emma turned and led the seven princesses up the dais. The 112 candles that lined the beautiful 4-layer star cake were color-coded. There were 7 colors and 16 of each color. That way every princess got 16 candles to blow out. It was a yellow cake with chocolate frosting and a pretty trellis running up both sides to meet at the top, where there were seven princess figurines riding through a meadow and onto a castle drawbridge. The castle looked a lot like their house—except for the drawbridge— with turrets and towers, balconies and windows, and beautiful stone walls. Emma looked out over the sea of people as the announcer did his thing. She caught Jake's eye and wondered where he had gotten the notion that her name was Emmaralda, and why did it sound so familiar?

Selena pondered Caleb's words. Had their father really sent him? Did he really love her or had he pretended to love her on her father's orders? 'Tania seemed to think he was lying about their father. Of course she had always been tender about that. 'Tania loved to do anything that made the wind rush through her hair: bike riding, horseback riding, boat rides, and running. Boy could she run. Sometimes it seemed like she wished she had a father so he could do these activities with her. Instead, she did them alone or with one of her sisters. Selena always loved to ride with her. Someday 'Tania would come out of her shell of independence and stop hating anyone who mentioned her father. But Selena could bet dollars to doughnuts that 'Tania would also think Caleb had lied about loving Selena. The trance surrounding Selena's thoughts broke as the crowd started counting.

"Ten…nine…eight…seven…six…five…four… three… two… one. HAPPY BIRTHDAY!" The words were screamed through the rafters as a warm sea wind blew through the room and encircled the seven princesses. It felt like they were being lifted up in this invisible boat. Then the sensation was gone, but each girl felt stronger and more in tune with herself. They felt like they could do whatever they wanted to with no problem.

A cry went up, 'Tania looked over to the dark wooden oak doors that had blown open. Men, dirty, smelly, tattooed men with bandannas and swords were running across the floor.

"Uhh… mom?" she asked.

"Queen Emmaralda, grab your daughters and run for the door! I'll hold them off," Caleb shouted, he ran to the nearest suit of armor and pulled a sword out of the knight's sheath before turning and engaging one of the more beastly looking men. "The pirates are after the princesses. Take them to the van I'll meet you there."

"Did he say pirates?" 'Tania had to yell to be heard over the commotion.

"Come on girls, you heard him. Let's go!" Emma was terrified at the memory that came back when Caleb shouted her name. She had finally realized why it was familiar. 17 years ago on her wedding day a powerful, evil dictator had taken over Faerie. A year later, Emmaralda and Thíshién, Emmaralda's husband, were negotiating when the dictators' men had thrown Emmaralda through the portal to the mortal world. That's when the car had hit her. Emmaralda now knew she had to find a way back to Thíshién.

"Mom, why are they here? Why are they after us?" Bella screamed. She looked like she was about to collapse from fright. "Why did he call you Emmaralda?"

"I'll explain everything in the van. Just run!" Emmaralda was scared the girls wouldn't listen. The sisters took one last look at the pirates and they all started running toward the door together. Caleb could be seen following them at a much slower pace as he tried to hold back the pirates, he was now fighting with two swords, the one he had grabbed from the suit of armor and another that he had taken from a pirate. As he reached the door, the seven princesses and the queen slammed it on the burly pirates. The door was half a foot thick and made of oak. It would keep the pirates held up for a while. The party ran to the van and started driving.

Chapter 3

_____ Explanation_____

"So you're taking us to a Faerie kingdom?" Autumn asked, completely confused. The tale their mother just told made them think she was losing her mind.

"Yes, I'm taking you home, and according to your cousin Caleb, the portal should be around here somewhere." Emmaralda turned to Caleb. "Right?"

"Yes, the portal's just around the corner. We have to make sure we all step through at the same time so none of us get left behind." _Otherwise those pirates_, Caleb thought to himself, _will kill that person._

"So we are about to go meet our real father in a fairy tale kingdom where we are all princesses, we're going to be chased by pirates for all eternity... And Caleb's our _cousin_?" 'Tania was positive her mother was losing her mind to believe the fantasies of Caleb. His name had been Jake and he had been a normal kid for the past two months that they had known him. Then out of the blue he said he knew their father and _bam_—their mother trusted him to lead them to a mythical place that didn't exist. It was completely insane. How could such a marvelous evening turn into such a frightening experience in which they had to run away from danger with insane people?

"Theoretically the pirates shouldn't be able to follow us into Faerie. I'm not even sure who they are... I mean, I knew you guys were vulnerable to attack after you turned 16 but I didn't expect it to happen so soon. I wonder how they got here and who put them up to it." Caleb lapsed into silence temporarily.

"And technically I was your adopted cousin, got orphaned again, and am now your adopted brother." Caleb knew 'Tania didn't believe him and was trying hard not to let her mom know it, but her act was slipping the more frightened she got. Or perhaps the more insane she thought they were.

"How could you not know what we had to face in Faerie? Didn't you just come from there?" *Great! Now Demy was starting to doubt him too. This would be some night.*

Emma looked back at Selena. She hadn't said anything since the pirates. Emma knew Selena felt betrayed by Caleb, and probably a little creeped out from Caleb's claim that he was their brother. She kept calling Caleb the girls' cousin. "You know Caleb was adopted by your uncle when he was a week old, and fostered by your father when your uncle died. Thíshién must have adopted him after I got lost in the mortal world," Selena responded, but not in the way Emmaralda expected.

"Do you hear that?" Selena whispered. In the background—very faintly but getting louder—was the sound of metal clashing and yelling. It was the pirates, and they were getting closer with every second. Just then the engine bucked and died. The sisters looked at each other.

"Everybody out of the van! We have to run the rest of the way." Emmaralda couldn't hide her fear for the kids, so she didn't. They all scrambled out of the van door as the first pirate rounded the corner. Caleb took the lead as

18

the group ran for their lives.

"How far?" 'Tania panted.

"Two blocks," Caleb responded as he whirled around and stabbed the lead pirate, who had reached their heels. 'Tania jumped as a pirate swung his sword towards her legs. Beside her Selena tripped over the uneven ground. A pirate grinned mercilessly and brought his blade down.

Clang.

Selena scrambled to her feet as Caleb's sword intercepted the pirate. She sprinted for her sisters. They had reached the last hill.

"At the top of the hill, wait until we're hand in hand," Caleb shouted over his shoulder. "We have to go through together."

'Tania reached the peak of the hill first. She gasped for breath and caught Demy's hand as she too reached the hill. They watched as the rest of the girls and their mother reached the top. Caleb was running now, no longer concerned with keeping the pirates at bay.

Caleb shouted as a pirate's blade whistled through the air and slit his arm open halfway up the bicep. Caleb's sword flew out of that hand and landed five feet away from him. Emmaralda ran back down the hill and grabbed it as the pirates closed in on Caleb.

"Get away from him!" she yelled as she swung the sword around in circles and injured the front pirates. Caleb jumped to his feet, wiping blood off his lip as he did so.

"Go!" he shouted as he took his sword back and sprinted up the hill to grab December's hand.

He waited until Emmaralda grabbed Selena's hand.

"On three!" Caleb shouted to the group as the pirates were halfway up the hill. They only had seconds before the pirates hit them. "One...two..." The pirates were swinging their swords. "Three!" The seven girls, Caleb, and Emmaralda stepped forward through the purple swirling portal and into Faerie.

Chapter 4

_____ Faerie_____

'Tania looked around. Lush green grass and wild purple flowers met her eyes. In the distance she saw trees.

"These are the Dynasty Meadows," Caleb said as he walked up behind 'Tania and her sisters. "Turn around." As one, the seven princesses turned and looked down the ridge at the beautiful flowing landscape. There, lying by the sea, was the most beautiful white structure the girls had ever seen. "Behold!" Caleb boomed, "The Castle of Kër Læil." The castle spread for at least a mile along the seashore, with miniature aqueducts forming bridges along the rivers that snaked through the castle's walls and towers. There were twelve towers rising above the walls. Five of them had pennants flying from the top. The meadow they were in stretched all the way to the castle moat. The castle had a definite air of majestic power. The white-washed sea walls that surrounded the interior castle had a feeling of magic that emanated from them.

As they watched, the sun rose over the highest tower, bathing the princesses in its warm light. 'Tania shielded her eyes. When they left, it had been night. Now dawn was breaking, the crystal light shining down on the beautiful land.

'Tania walked forward and smelled the salty air. "I feel like I'm home." All the princesses felt a pull toward the castle and a peaceful feeling that everything would be all right.

"We are, 'Tania. We're finally home," Emmaralda said, as she spun around before breaking into a run with her seven daughters. The lost princesses had returned with their queen.

The castle walls came closer as the eight raced forward. Caleb wasn't running. Over the main bridge there was a light held by a man in his early thirties.

"Em-Emmaralda," Thíshién stuttered.

"Thíshién!" Emmaralda raced forward and embraced her husband while 'Tania, Selena, and their sisters slowed and stood, unsure what to do. "I've missed you so! How is everything?"

"The dictator is gone, if that's what you mean. The country was saddened by your loss but now that you're back it will thrive more than ever," Thíshién said with feeling.

'Tania finally got a good look at this man, who was apparently the one claiming to be their father. He was tall and imposing, but there was an air of friendliness about him. His black hair framed his pale face and blue eyes. He looked a lot like Caleb, only taller and aged. She didn't know why she felt so uncomfortable. All she ever wanted was a father to hug and be with. If only he had come with them to the mortal world maybe then things would have been better. 'Tania looked at Selena. She looked like their dad in some ways, with dark brown hair and similar facial features. The only weird thing was her eyes. They weren't blue, they were brown. But that was normal in people, wasn't it? Whoever heard of someone with dark hair and blue eyes? It had to be rare. *It must be a Faerie thing*, 'Tania thought. Thíshién turned and looked at the girls standing at the edge of the drawbridge.

"Oh my word." Thíshién seemed to gasp. "I'd hoped for years my child lived, and look! Seven—just like the prophecy said." Thíshién didn't care that he sounded like a fool, he just knew that his family was home. He walked forward a little staring at the girls. "Wow, wow, you all look so much like your mother and me. Oh you guys are probably dying to see your home. Come, I must show you the castle."

"Yes, it looks different than when I was last here." Emmaralda stepped back and tried to find some similarity between the old castle and the new one.

"I had it remodeled after the war left the original in ruins." Thíshién spoke without emotion, but one could see he wished Emmaralda would love it.

"Well then, I think you better show us the layout," Emmaralda said, her face breaking into a smile as she took Thíshién's hand and led him across the drawbridge.

"Do you believe this?" Demy asked her sisters as they followed their parents into the castle grounds.

"I don't, but Mom obviously does. Do you think she's finally lost it?" December asked, bashful to suggest that their mother was insane.

"As much as I hate to admit it, some of us do look a lot like him," Selena commented in an undertone. "I mean, he obviously knows our mom even if he may or may not be our father."

"Another thing is this place, I mean it's clearly not in California. It's not a huge stretch to say it's in a different universe or world or whatever. I mean we sound crazy but we can see this place, its real." Milæyka said looking around with some doubt.

23

"Well, if what he says is true, then the date we disappeared should be our birthday, right?" 'Tania asked. "And where did that jerk go?"

"You mean Caleb? He went around the side of castle, I think he said something about getting his arm looked at." Bella said, coming into the conversation.

"I don't trust him," 'Tania said with disgust. She acted like saying his name was a deadly curse that ruined all in sight.

"Well, I do, 'Tania," December said, glancing at Selena to see how she felt. After all, he had lied the most to her.

"What about you, Selena? Do you still… trust him?" Demy asked quietly, not sure she should include "like him."

"I don't know… I'm confused." Selena turned, trying to restrain the tears that threatened to overflow her eyes.

"Girls! Come on, if you don't pay attention you will get lost in the castle." Emmaralda turned to Thíshién and saw him smile at the girls in an amused manner.

"They do not believe yet," Thíshién commented to Emmaralda as they continued walking through the entrance courtyard.

"They'll come around."

Thíshién turned his back to the castle as they reached the end of the entrance courtyard. "Follow me, and I'll show my unique feature of this castle." Thíshién took a quick right to the skinny set of stone stairs built into the side of a battlement overlooking the courtyard. As he climbed the stairs he grew more encouraged by the looks on the girls' faces. "Behold the tower expanse." The girls gasped as they came around the last steps, for instead of an overview of the entire inner castle, there was nothing but ceiling! Or floor, whichever way you looked at it. Flowerpots and benches broke the expanse of concrete.

"Do you like it?"

"Like it? I love it, Thíshién! Whatever made you think of a courtyard on the roof?" Emmaralda was so proud of her husband. The odd thing about the courtyard was the 12 towers rising at even intervals and the large holes occupying some areas. "What are the holes for?"

"The holes are courtyards on the lower level. The towers are bedrooms. I had seven refurnished for the princesses and assigned them by age. On my layout they appear as daughter one's tower and so on."

"So we each have our own tower? What are the others for?" Autumn asked quizzically.

"One tower is mine, one is your mother's. For space of course, only my tower has a full bed. Your mother has a small bed for naps. One tower is Caleb's, and one is your hangout tower, princesses only."

"That's only eleven. I see twelve towers." 'Tania pointed out.

"Oh yes, the other is, ummm…" Thíshién looked uncomfortable and started shifting from side to side. He started to speak, then stopped as a young girl came running up to him.

"Dad! There you are. I got back from my visit to Kër Wælakor and no one knew where you had gone." She turned, noticing the group assembled. "Who are they?"

"Ummm… well you see, this is Emmaralda."

"Your lost wife?" the girl looked to Thíshién in surprise.

"Yes, as you can see she is no longer lost, however," Thíshién said, obviously even more uncomfortable than before.

"Well obviously, she is no longer lost if she's standing here. But who are the others? I thought you only had one kid by Emmaralda." The girl obviously used sarcasm a lot by the look on Thíshién's face.

25

"Thíshién, who is this?" Emmaralda looked at Thíshién sharply.

"Okay, one at a time. This is Princess Melody, she is my adopted daughter. The twelfth tower is hers. Melody, Emmaralda was only pregnant once by me, these are your septuplet sisters, all born at the same time. Their names are… How could I have not asked your names?" Thíshién looked deeply concerned that he had forgotten that.

"My name is Milæyka, I was first born."

"My name is Selena, I was second," she said in a monotone.

"My name is Demy, I was third." Demy nudged 'Tania when she didn't speak up.

"My name is 'Tania, I was fourth." 'Tania said with a sigh. She didn't see the point in introducing themselves to their father.

"My name is December, I was fifth."

"My name is Autumn, I was sixth."

"And I'm Bella, I am the youngest."

"Pleased to meet you guys. I'm 12."

"We are 16," Bella replied.

Emmaralda finally recovered her voice, "Thíshién, why didn't you say you had adopted a princess?"

"She wasn't a princess when I adopted her, understand. You know it's tradition to adopt a young one from a surrounding orphanage if you're royalty." Thíshién looked sheepishly at Emmaralda.

Melody was young with blond hair and a slight body. Her face was happy, and standing in a dark blue gown, her blond hair with a blue and green streak clearly emphasized her facial features. The one odd thing was her eyes. They were slightly slanted and they changed color whenever she moved. Her fingernails also seemed to be like that. "Why didn't you tell them about me?" Melody asked her father as she rounded on him, clearly annoyed. Then the

26

miraculous happened. As Melody got more annoyed at her father for his stuttered answers, Melody's streak in her hair turned bright yellow, almost losing itself in her hair. The princesses gawked in amazement. "What are you all staring at?" Melody had noticed the princesses looking at her.

"Your hair...it...it..."

"Changed colors," Melody finished Demy's amazed and stuttered answer. "Honestly, why do people stare at that so much? They act as if they had never seen a land mermaid."

"We haven't... but what's a land mermaid?" Selena asked.

"A land mermaid is a mermaid who is fully functional on land, but who can turn into a mermaid at will when in the water," Melody said, as if everyone should know this.

Emmaralda looked at Thíshién with obvious surprise etched into her face. She led him off into the interior of the castle, asking him questions in an undertone.

"Well, so much for our tour," 'Tania said sarcastically, as she watched the two get sucked into the enveloping darkness of the castle.

"Melody, could you show us our towers?" December asked.

"Sure thing, just let me get the map that tells me whose is whose." Melody ran off and returned with a roll of parchment, which she rolled out in front of her. "As you can see, we are on the north side of the castle. The three closest towers belong to 'Tania, December, and Selena. Facing the castle, 'Tania's is in the middle, Selena's is on the right, and December's is on the left. Now if you will follow me, I will lead you to the towers' doors and then show you the next couple."

"Hold on—before you do, why are our names on that if he didn't know our names till a few minutes ago?"

"Simple—before I grabbed it I substituted the daughter

numbers with the names of the princesses. I think I got them all correct. We will figure out if I was wrong when we get there. Now come on."

"How could you possibly remember?" 'Tania looked at Melody incredulously.

"You guys were standing in that order at the time. Plus I have a really good memory." Melody replied.

'Tania turned to Selena and said under her breath, "This girl is crazy!"

Selena laughed, 'Tania, just because she has a great memory does not make her a psycho."

"Could you do that Selena?"

"No, 'Tania, I couldn't, but she's not even human…"

"I also have great hearing." Melody called behind her shoulder.

'Tania and Selena looked at each other embarrassed.

The group reached a tower with a plaque on it reading "daughter four." "'Tania, you are daughter four, right?"

"Yeah, I am," 'Tania answered in a stiff manner, annoyed and still embarrassed Melody had heard her conversation with Selena.

"Well, this is your tower. There is a greatly detailed map in the tower that will help you find your way around the castle. It will be way more detailed than the map I am using now to find your towers." Melody watched 'Tania ascend the stairs as she turned to the group again and had them follow her to the next tower, Selena's.

When Melody was finished matching her new sisters to the appropriate towers she went to her own and sighed. She now not only had lost her father to a new mother, but she had to share him with seven sisters as well. Oh well, some of them liked her and treated her as one of them. Melody looked out her tower window at the hustle and bustle of the castle, and then sat at her desk to make a new pennant for her tower. Now that she was the eighth daughter, things were bound to change.

Chapter 5

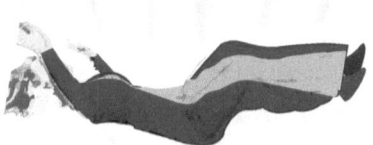

_____ 'Tania's Power_____

'Tania's tower was octagonal and very bare. There was a four-poster bed with royal blue hangings, a royal blue comforter and pale pink sheets. A little table in the corner was covered with an assortment of papers; some were new and crisp while others were so yellowed and crumpled 'Tania was afraid to touch them. There were maps of various quality and outlook, papers on the history of the kingdom, a list of furniture and décor she could request for her room, and a poem sitting on top of a stack of books. The window to the right side of the bed was set into a wide alcove that could probably contain a window seat. 'Tania looked around again and spotted a royal blue fabric on the bed that blended in with the comforter. At a closer look it was a flag. On top of it was a note reading, "When you figure out the meaning of the pennant, fly it from the top of your tower." The pennant was royal blue, with a royal blue unicorn outlined in pale pink. 'Tania turned and brought the pennant to the table. "One of these books has to have an answer," she mused out loud.

'Tania picked up the nearest book and read the title, _A Complete Guide to the Magical Creatures in Faerie_. _That ought to be fun_, 'Tania thought as she set it down and picked up the next couple of books. _Royal History of the Seven Kingdoms: Emblems, Family Trees and More_, and _Castle Construction: Past and Future_ looked helpful enough. 'Tania opened the first book and scanned the table of contents. "Pennants, pennants, pennants," she muttered under her breath. "Ah ha—pennants, how to mount and how they are decorated." 'Tania flipped to the page number and read the paragraph.

A royal family with multiple children will have each child fly a pennant from their window or tower. The pennant will have a simple family emblem in the right hand corner and a symbol for the child in question in the middle of the pennant. 'Tania looked at the pennant again. Sure enough, in the right hand corner there was a pale blue moon intertwining with a red sun. 'Tania turned the book page and studied some of the symbols they gave. They had the symbols for each of the seven faerie kingdoms and an explanation of why each one was which.

Every generation of royal persona is given a different type of symbol that corresponds in some way to who the person is. The first generation in a cycle is given a symbol that is a natural element, for example the sun, the moon, wind, stars, etc. The second generation will receive a symbol that looks like an animal, for example a cat, a dog, a horse, a wolf etc. The third generation receives a double symbol, similar to those representing kingdoms, except their symbol is their mom's and their grandmothers' symbols intertwined in a chain of the fathers and grandfathers symbols. For example, moon intertwined with a wolf, surrounded by a vine of alternating suns and rabbits.

"How, strange. I wonder what the others animals are... Only one way to find out," 'Tania said to herself as she closed the book. To get to the top of the tower, she would have to climb up the side of the roof and clip the flag to the pole. The prospect scared her, but there was no other way to get the pennant to the top. 'Tania walked out onto the balcony and looked up, surprised, as she saw a ladder leading up to another ledge that could be easily stood on to reach the pole the flag could be attached to. 'Tania smiled. This would be a piece of cake.

Climbing the ladder was easy; hanging the flag, not so easy. When 'Tania reached the ledge she could see her sisters doing the same thing on their respective towers and everything going on in the courtyard below; closest to 'Tania, there was a group of pre-teen boys playing a ball game. 'Tania waved to Selena and reached up to grab the hooks that would attach to the flag's corners. The wind was blowing hard, a young fairy on the floor/roof below threw a ball, 'Tania turned too late, the ball slammed into her side, and she lost her balance....

"'Tania!!" Selena yelled as she watched her sister fall from the tower. On the other side of 'Tania's tower December turned at Selena's scream and watched as 'Tania turned in midair and...hovered. Selena and December watched open-mouthed as 'Tania somehow managed to soar to the balcony on her tower.

"Ahhhhhhhhh!" was all 'Tania could think as she spiraled off the tower towards the concrete-looking surface below. She couldn't believe she was going to die now after surviving at birth and surviving the pirates. She wished she could stop falling. A sensation came over her body that felt

31

like somebody was pulling her up by her intestines. She slowed and stopped her descent, then started to rise. *What the…* 'Tania thought as she soared to her balcony and landed. *Did I just fly back up the tower?* For a girl who had just been chased by pirates, found out she was a princess in a mystical land, and met a father she had never heard of, 'Tania thought she was pretty much done with strange occurrences. Boy, was she wrong. Emmaralda came running up the tower steps and burst into the room, with Thíshién close behind.

"Sweetie, are you okay?" Emma asked as she embraced her daughter tightly.

"I'm fine, Mom, really. Just a little freaked." 'Tania was a lot freaked, but she didn't want her mom to know it.

"Thíshién! What is going on?" Emmaralda turned on her husband again. You could tell he was nervous.

"Well, you see, there's this prophecy that suggests that septuplets born in the mortal world would each have a special power, but one would be more special then them all and they would have to save the kingdom from a nameless evil," Thíshién blurted out quickly. He had hoped to break the news gently and when everyone was happy. That hope was gone.

Emmaralda turned white as a sheet as she looked back at 'Tania, then at the door where the other princesses were gathering. "You mean each of my daughters has a special power?" She turned to 'Tania. "Yours must be flight," she muttered, "Thíshién, what is this evil?" Emmaralda asked, turning back around.

"I don't know. All I know is the prophecy and the legend that says ancient monsters will awaken at the turn of the century." Thíshién bowed his head and looked sideways at the table with all the books on it. "I put a copy of the prophecy in that pile somewhere."

Emmaralda walked over to the table and picked up the poem that lay on top of a pile of books.

"In a time of superb danger,
through the portal a loved one falls
In mortal world, when struck by car,
of Faeire she cannot recall
Seven daughters born with powers,
together triumph over death
Daughter one with persuasive tongue
can snap and be obeyed
Daughter two when concentrating,
is invisible, telepath
Daughter three constructs destroys,
things of rock, sand and stone remade
Daughter four with powers of flight
upon the changing winds can ride
Daughter five with little effort,
can manipulate the weather
Daughter six is complicated;
the laws of nature are defied
Daughter seven talks to animals,
with skin and fur and feather
The princesses together joined in song
can bring down even stone
The seven daughters of the king,
will conquer monsters, New Years brings
At age sixteen their powers come,
when at midnight a warm wind's blown
They are sought by the evil,
who'll lose the fight against the siblings
One of the seven has one more power,
and she will be the key
Worlds and distance are meaningless,
but she must thrive through ignorance"

She stayed quiet for a long time, just staring at the parchment, then without warning she left the tower with tears flowing down her face.

"Mom?" Bella asked as Emmaralda descended the staircase. Emmaralda waved her hand dismissively as she shut the tower door.

"I'll talk to her, girls, don't worry. Why don't you guys go explore? You could go to the pool or the stables; the map on the table and the wall will give you fairly good directions." And with those parting words Thíshién swept out of the tower.

The girls huddled around the table and read the prophecy, each finding what their power was supposed to be. After trying the powers unsuccessfully, the girls looked at the map and each found a destination. 'Tania found her way to the stables where she found Melody grooming a lovely dappled mare with a white stockings, a white star and stripe, and a flowing black mane and tail. 'Tania leaned against the stall partition and stared at the majestic beast. "Wow! That's a really nice horse."

Melody whipped around, startled. "Oh," she exclaimed in surprise, "I didn't see you there. This is Claro de Luna Armonía."

"What does that mean? Is it Spanish?" 'Tania loved the sound of the horse's singsong name.

"Literally it means Clear of Moon Harmony. However, in English we tend to say Moonlight's Harmony." Melody smiled as she finished grooming Moonlight's Harmony. "I call her Luna." She stepped out of the horse's stall and shut the bolt. "Would you like to see your horse?"

"I have my very own horse?" 'Tania knew her mouth was hanging open, but she couldn't seem to shut it. "How...."

"Our father is very influential. He found seven five-year-olds. All very well bred. He knew there would be one or seven of you depending on whether or not you guys were the kids in the prophecy, so he went ahead and got seven of everything just in case." Melody smirked as if she thought her father was a little extreme. "Anyway, he bought each horse based on color, gender, and name, trying to match up each of you with a horse related to your power, since he didn't know your names."

"Oh, I get it. Like you horse is named Moonlight's Harmony, and your name is Melody. Harmony, Melody, that makes sense." 'Tania thought it was clever to make the horses personalized even if it was a little weird. "How will I know which one mine is?"

"I'll show you the row with the seven horses and their names. I think you can figure which ones which yourself." Melody laughed, "Of course if you can't manage I guess I could give you *some* hints…" Melody continued walking around a corner, and went through a low-rise door. As 'Tania followed her through the seemingly secret door, she held her breath. For there in front of her was a row of horses all sleek and beautiful like racehorses. Their names were engraved on the stall doors. 'Tania whispered them to herself as she walked forward.

"Persuasive Reason, Mind Reader, Emerald Isle, Skye, Elemental Beauty, Season Coming, Animal Call." 'Tania looked up and was immediately drawn to the horse in the center. "Skye," 'Tania whispered. She looked over at Melody and asked, "Is Skye my horse?"

"Yup. Look closer and see why." Melody tried to suppress her grin as 'Tania walked forward in a trance to look at Skye.

"She's blue!" 'Tania said in surprise. "And she has wings!"

"You noticed," Melody said with a slight smirk. "Skye is a Terra Pegasus—if you touch the wings your hand goes right through them," Melody swung her hand through the holographic wings. "But you can see them and they work." Melody came to stand beside 'Tania as she explained where Skye had come from and who she was.

"Wow, she's beautiful," 'Tania said. "I'll have to find one of my sisters so we can ride together." 'Tania turned to leave, then added, "You can come too if you want."

"No, that's okay. I have to go to my classes," Melody responded indifferently.

'Tania was briefly taken aback. "Yes, I suppose even in Faerie kids have to go to school," she said, more to herself than to Melody. "Well, see you later then." And with that 'Tania turned and left the stables in search of Selena.

❄ ❄ ❄ ❄ ❄

Selena looked up as 'Tania came around the corner of the courtyard. She knew with one glance that 'Tania had discovered something she thought was awesomely cool. Selena sighed inwardly and than smiled as she stood and went to meet her sister halfway. "Hey 'Tania. What did you find?" Selena asked trying to sound cheerful.

'Tania looked at Selena critically then responded, "Our 'father' bought us each our very own horse to ride!" 'Tania suddenly burst out with a huge grin. "Mine is light blue with a white mane and tail and holographic wings! Her name is Skye. You have to come on a ride with me— these horses are amazing. They look like pure thoroughbreds!" 'Tania was practically bouncing up and down with the exciting prospect of riding through Dynasty Meadows. Selena looked unsure. "Come on! We can look at the surrounding area and maybe meet some of our subjects." Selena laughed and agreed to follow 'Tania to the stables. "Goody!" 'Tania raced across the courtyard and stood waiting. "Are you coming or not?" she said, exasperated.

"All right, all right." Selena laughed once more and hurried to catch up to her sister.

❄ ❄ ❄ ❄ ❄

'Tania stopped suddenly at the brink of another courtyard. "Selena, stop!" she called, but it was too late. Selena rounded the bend and saw why 'Tania had stopped. She let out a cry of shock, for there in front of her was Caleb kissing a petite brunette with fair skin and a skimpy dress. His head was bent down towards her and they looked like the only two people on the planet, but at Selena's cry he looked up and stared.

"Wait!" he yelled, but Selena took off running back the way she came, not caring where she went, just trying to get away. 'Tania took one more look at the girl in Caleb's arms and took off after her.

Chapter 6

_____Thíshién's Idea_____

Selena looked like a stone statue as she lay across her bed. Her bed was identical to 'Tania's except the canopy and comforter were midnight blue and the sheets were pale yellow. Selena was pale. "I was such a fool. No wonder he always seemed so reserved on our dates. He already had a girlfriend." She turned over onto her back.

'Tania had been listening to this over and over again and was just about ready to storm out of there, find Caleb, and give him a firm punch in the mouth. "Remember what Milæyka said? She said 'boys aren't worth the trouble.' And she's right! Selena, you gotta pull out of this. Pretend you don't care. If he ever had an inkling of feeling for you it might show through jealousy. He'll be jealous that you don't even care that he was cheating on you." 'Tania looked at her sister in despair.

"'Tania, even if he does want me back I don't know if I can trust him. Ever. He cheated on me for two months and he lied about his entire life. If he knew our father, why didn't he say something two months ago?" Selena was beyond despair at this point. She had no tears left and no emotion in her voice, and then she was suddenly indignant. "Hey! That's not nice," she said, "You wanted to comfort me after all."

"Selena, what are you talking about?" 'Tania asked, as she turned back around towards Selena. "I didn't say anything... Where are you?" 'Tania looked at the bed where her sister was supposed to be, and wasn't.

"What are you talking about, 'Tania? I heard you talk and I'm still in the same place I was a moment ago!" Selena got off the bed to go touch 'Tania, who was looking around as if wondering where her voice was coming from. "'Tania, I'm right here," Selena said as she grabbed 'Tania's arm and pulled. 'Tania let out an ear-piercing shriek. "'Tania! Shut up!" Selena screamed over her.

'Tania recovered her voice and let out a squeak, "What was your power again?" Selena, finally understanding, went over to the table in the corner of her bedchamber and grabbed the piece of parchment. She read it, then handed it to 'Tania at a loss of words. "You can turn invisible and you're telepathic." 'Tania read off the sheet. She turned pale than started to rise off the ground and float towards the ceiling. "Oh!" she exclaimed and fell ten feet back to the ground. She moaned as Selena, now visible, rushed over to her. "Did you know that on the top of your canopy there's the symbol that's on your flag?" 'Tania asked randomly. Selena rolled her eyes and started to say something when their other five sisters came in.

"King Thíshién of Faerie requested an audience with the seven princesses in front of his advisors and some of the top knights," Milæyka said with equal airs of annoyance at being a messenger and nerves at being called in front so many government officials. 'Tania and Selena lifted themselves off the floor and they all went out the door to find the Meeting Hall, which according to the map was at the far end of the castle where there was no rooftop courtyard, right next to the Great Hall.

❄ ❄ ❄ ❄ ❄

The seven princesses rounded the doorway to see their mother and "father" embraced in a passionate kiss. They looked around at the advisors and knights, all of whom were trying not to look. "Um... excuse me?" December asked to no response, "Mom?" Still nothing. "Okay. On the count of three, 1...2...3 MOM!" The sisters yelled in chorus. The two looked up and blushed.

"Um...right, then." Thíshién started as he cleared his throat and looked around the room. "Well, I called you all here on the matter of my newly found wife and our teenage girls." He looked down the aisle and smiled at the girls. "So far 'Tania is the only one with discovered powers... Ah yes 'Tania."

"Selena just discovered her powers as well."

"Oh. Well then, let me change that," Thíshién said. "So far only 'Tania *and Selena* have found their powers. I propose we train these maidens and send them to see the Ancient One in Arcadia once they have all found their powers."

'Tania raised her hand. "Don't we get a say in this?" she asked indignantly.

Thíshién rolled his eyes and sighed. "We will vote. All in favor of the princesses seeing the Ancient One raise their hands." Over half the gathering raised their hands; Emmaralda and her daughters abstained.

"Thíshién—I've asked you a hundred times and I'll ask again—isn't there another way?" Emmaralda knew what the Ancient One was and had no wish to send her daughters across miles of difficult terrain to see it.

41

"No. I looked for the answers for sixteen years while you were stuck in the mortal world, Emma. It's not there. But don't worry. The girls cannot be sent out until they complete the training test, plus I will send Caleb with them. He will not let us down."

Thíshién was getting tired of his plans being dissed. He was king; he knew best. Why was his judgment being questioned? Thíshién looked around the room to find Caleb and realized one crucial point. Caleb wasn't in the meeting hall. Opening his mouth to say something, Thíshién stopped when a gesture caught his eye. Thíshién looked around the brightly lit hall again and saw it again. Caleb was gesturing frantically towards him from the one dark corner.

"Here is Caleb now to show you seven to your first lesson—sword fighting. Emmaralda and I shall retire to my tower to continue our discussion. Everyone else, back to whatever I told you to do before I told you to come here." And with that last confusing statement, Thíshién stood, swept his cloak around the throne, and he and Emmaralda left the meeting hall.

Caleb looked at the seven girls waiting in front of him. Selena's eyes were red while 'Tania's were full of hatred. Feeling guilty, Caleb refused to meet the eyes of either one of them, and instead stared at the floor where he noticed, to his amusement, that there was a mistake in the tile pattern. With this newfound knowledge clearing his head, Caleb looked up and gestured to the princesses to follow him. Their first lesson was with the new sword master, Sir Drakôn. The sword training took place on the roof, near Caleb's tower.

✽ ✽ ✽ ✽ ✽

The sisters huddled together behind Caleb, following him to the sword-fighting lesson. They talked to each other every now and then, commenting on bits of the castle they hadn't seen before, and marveling at the spectacular views from the roof. Upon reaching the arena where they would be taught, the princesses ceased their conversations and looked around.

"Where is Sir Drakôn?" December asked, scanning the sword arena. "I don't see anyone."

Caleb smirked and let out a weird yodel that sounded like a dying badger. "Sir Drakôn is a busy person who will only come when absolutely needed. Hence the call," Caleb said, not wanting to receive any sarcastic remarks from the princesses. "He is highly trained and is an expert in his field. In fact, here he comes now." Caleb tried to hide a smile as the sword instructor came into view.

A teenage boy around 17 years of age walked up the steps from the sun yard, the center courtyard, his blond hair flipping in the slight wind, and his unbuttoned shirt flowing behind him as he walked. He was your class A Californian surfer dude. The boy came to a stop in front of Milæyka.

"Hello, I'm Talon." Talon smiled as he reached out his hand to take Milæyka's. "I have the fortune of teaching you all your first lesson today.

"You!" Milæyka blurted out. "You're our age! What a joke. We are waiting for Sir Drakôn. You cannot teach us anything!"

Talon smirked and smiled at Caleb. Then he stepped towards Milæyka and held up his sword. "Wanna bet?" he asked with a slight smile.

Milæyka smirked back. She and her sisters had been taught how to sword fight over the last couple of years from their mother's boss. Milæyka had been the best. As a response to Talon's question, she grabbed Caleb's sword from his scabbard and held it in front of her vertically.

As soon as Milæyka was ready, Talon attacked.

43

Boy could he fight! He jabbed at Milæyka three times and pinned her to the ground. "Again!" she yelled.

Once again Talon came at Milæyka. She met his swinging blade with a hard block while she tried to sidestep and cut a nick in his shoulder, but Talon's foot appeared under hers and Milæyka crashed to the ground. Talon jumped over her and placed his sword point over her heart.

"Gotcha!" he said in a boastful manner. The six princesses on the sidelines tried to hide their laughter as Talon helped Milæyka to her feet. "Allow me to introduce myself formally. I am Sir Talon Drakôn and I will be your instructor for the next few weeks." Talon laughed as the seven princesses mouths dropped open and stayed there. Talon put his arm around Milæyka, "Thank you for allowing me to make a fool of you for our demonstration. I am glad you're sweet on me."

Milæyka sent him a look that clearly could have burnt holes in him if he had noticed. "*Sweet* on *YOU!*" she exclaimed. She shrugged his arm off and attacked him with a new ferocity. "Nay sir," she said as she overcame him. "I was merely preparing you for this righteous beating." Milæyka let a surprised-looking Talon up and he dusted himself off.

"Uhh…right then." Talon gave her a one last look of surprise and started his instruction on how to surprise your enemy with random, but systematic sword fighting. "The key is to always be thinking ahead and to watch your opponent keenly," he began as he started a fake fight with Caleb. "Plan your attacks to counteract your opponent's and give you the advantage at the same time. I tell you this because according to your father, you know basic swordplay. Judging by Milæyka's performance, you had a good teacher."

"What would he know?" Milæyka muttered to her sister. "He beat me easily, the jerk."

Selena and 'Tania gave non-committal grunts while the others just ignored Milæyka. Milæyka rolled her eyes and continued watching the mock fight. Both boys had taken their shirts off, probably because it was around 80° out. Though the more Milæyka thought about it, the more she saw other reasons. *I swear Talon is flirting with me*, she thought as she studied his footwork and hand positioning. "Jerk," Milæyka muttered out loud as she watched Talon finally pin Caleb down.

"Now it's your turn." Talon rolled a metal barrel full of swords in front of the girls. "Divide into groups. Milæyka will spar with me, Selena with Caleb, 'Tania with Demy, and December with Autumn. Bella will help whoever seems to need it."

Chapter 7

_____Lessons_____

Years later 'Tania would always remember their first sword fighting lesson. And it wasn't just because of the pair mix-ups. That's an understatement. The pairs weren't mixed up—they were disastrous. Selena was trying to behead Caleb while Milæyka was trying to injure Talon to the point of hospitalization. If Bella hadn't been paying close attention to all the fights to figure out who needed help, things could have gotten really nasty. As it was, Talon had to have stitches in his head, Milæyka had to get stitches in her arm, Selena had to be hospitalized briefly to make sure she hadn't lost too much blood from a gash in her leg, and Caleb was nursing a black eye and a gash across his chest. Thíshién was furious. He had banned use of steel swords from any of the princesses, Talon, and Caleb until the princesses became knights. 'Tania could only hope that the princesses' first horseback ride together would go more smoothly.

❄ ❄ ❄ ❄ ❄

"They're beautiful," Milæyka said as she pet her horse. "And such a pretty name." Her horse, Persuasive Reason, was a jet-black mare with one white spot on her forehead.

Selena looked over Mind Reader's back and smiled. Mind Reader was what Selena had always wanted—a white mare with a black mane and tail. She was the picture of loveliness. "It's amazing how each horse reflects our personality. It must have been a lot of work to find them. They seem to be the best of their breeds."

The horses were indeed the very best. Demy's horse, Emerald Isle, was green with a white mane and tail and a white stripe. December's horse, Elemental Beauty, was a palomino mare. Golden with a white mane and tail, she had a white star and stripe as well as white hooves.

Autumn came into the room-like stable with a saddle over her arm and a bridle on one shoulder. "Season Coming," she read as she walked over to her horse's stall. "Whoa! She looks like a cat!" Autumn yelled as she leaned over the stall partition then jumped back.

"Seriously?" December asked, coming over to look. "Hey, she's right—this horse is calico colored."

The other five princesses came over to look. "Weird," Bella said. "Animal Call is a plain chestnut." Animal Call was the only "normal" colored horse in the princesses' section of the barn.

"Yeah, but aren't most animals brown?" Selena asked.

"Good point," Bella replied, looking thoughtful.

"You guys ready yet?" Melody called from the doorway, holding the reins to Claro de Luna Armonía. "The instructor is becoming impatient."

"Yeah, we're coming," 'Tania called back. She grabbed Skye's reins and headed towards the door. "Who's our instructor? It isn't another person our age, is it?"

"Don't worry. I think Dad's afraid to give you another

instructor your age." Melody let out a small laugh. "This one's roughly our parents' age." Melody left the doorway as 'Tania led Skye through it. "This way," she said leading the way down to a grassy fenced-in plain.

"Don't you hate it when she says our parents." Milæyka muttered to Demy and Selena as she joined the procession of princesses. Demy and Selena both made different non-committal noises.

✳ ✳ ✳ ✳ ✳

"Okay. Now, your father has told me that you all have experience on horseback. This first "lesson" will primarily be small warm-up exercises that will let you get to know your horses and start to build a bond." The instructor was a small woman in her thirties with light brown hair. The eight girls were mounted on their horses facing the woman. "My name is Genna. Any questions?" Genna waited for the space of three heartbeats. "No? Good. Our first exercise will be a simple equitation—well I wouldn't really call it a pattern necessarily..." Genna broke off for a moment, lost in thought. "Anyway, trot around the ring twice, do a figure eight, then canter around once. Melody, go first, then the rest of you follow in order." The princesses' "order" was the order they were born in.

Nothing exciting happened until Bella and Milæyka were coming straight at each other during the figure eight. *I get right of way! I get right of way!* Bella was screaming in her head, as the two horses got dangerously closer to each other. Persuasive Reason stopped and went the other way. Milæyka, who was at the time trying to get Reason to go the other way, turned around in the saddle and said very pointedly, "I didn't do that." Meanwhile Bella sat there, stunned.

"What's the matter, Bella?" Melody asked.

49

"I... don't know... let me try something." Bella thought really hard, *Persuasive Reason, buck Milæyka off, buck Milæyka off, BUCK MILÆYKA OFF!*

Milæyka flew off Reason's back with a thud as Reason took off galloping and bucking. Bella couldn't help herself; Milæyka looked so funny sitting in the dirt, Bella laughed. She laughed so hard she was in danger of falling off herself.

Milæyka watched Bella laughing and got really annoyed. Her vision started going red around the edges as the emotion welled up inside of her. Milæyka stalked forward with hatred burning in her eyes. Her hand came up as if to strike. A loud snap echoed around the grassy plain and Milæyka yelled one word, "STOP!" Bella stopped laughing like she had been choked.

'Tania let out a small whisper. "I think they've found their powers."

❋ ❋ ❋ ❋ ❋

After a week of various training, 'Tania decided that her favorite classes were sword fighting, horseback-riding, Faerie classes (classes that explained the world of Faerie to the girls), and power lessons. Some of her less favorite lessons included dancing, sewing, and etiquette. Power lessons were stressed the most by the princesses' teachers and by their father. At the end of the week, Demy, Autumn, and December still hadn't found their powers, and stress levels were running high in that class.

"Come on, guys! I know you can do it. Concentrate really hard on what you want to happen. December, make it rain; Demy make a wall from that pile of rocks; and Autumn, do whatever you think you should do." The instructor, Sir Kaill, was about to start cursing (in his mind) if these girls didn't get the hang of their powers soon.

"Give them a break, Kaill. Their powers seem harder

to decipher the meaning of from the prophecy. Maybe we should just stress them out or something," Milæyka said in her most flattering tone. Sir Kaill annoyed her to no end with his constantly cheery voice that hinted at desperation.

"*What?*" Sir Kaill asked in deep confusion.

"Milæyka's right, the rest of us have found our powers while experiencing a strong emotion. Maybe we should invoke strong emotions in them to let their powers show," 'Tania added.

"What do you plan on doing to us?" Demy asked, anger growing in her because the others were deciding her fate without her input.

Selena, sensing Demy's anger, replied, "Oh, I don't know. We could toss you guys off a cliff like 'Tania, we could put you on bucking broncos like Milæyka. Ooh! I know. We should lock you in the dungeon. I like that plan; I'll go get the keys." Selena turned around and began walking towards the castle (power lessons took place in Dynasty Meadows). Demy didn't know why, but rage was bubbling in her like a volcano.

As Selena passed the rock pile Demy was supposed to be transforming, Demy's rage boiled to a maximum and she started chanting a loud poem.

> "*Rock that sits there, sitting still*
> *Come to life, exercise your will*
> *Stop that girl, keep her here*
> *Hold her 'till I say 'all clear'*
> *Form a giant at my snap, stand up and do my bidding*
> *Hurry now, the girl in question is getting up and running*"

Demy finished her rhyme and snapped. Selena, who had broken into a run near the end of the rhyme, stopped and looked back as loud crunching noises echoed around the meadow. Demy stared at the rock pile as it started forming a person. The rocks piling on top of each other at odd angles until a seven-foot rock monster was formed. The monster looked around, its massive hand scratching its head, before spotting Selena who was backing slowly away from the gigantic monster, hyperventilating.

"Demy! We get it. You can make it stop now..." Selena screamed and ducked as the monster swiped a huge rock hand towards her head.

"I can't figure out how!" Demy screamed back her eyes squinted in frustration.

Autumn saw all this with a growing fear in her stomach. *The rock monster's going to kill Selena!* she thought over and over again. *What can I do? What harms rock? Erosion harms rock, but that takes years. The prophecy says I can defy natures laws, but does that mean I can speed up erosion?* Autumn stared at the rock and thought really hard.

> *Sand and wind swirl ever faster*
> *Create a whirling vortex*
> *Surround the rock and beat it down*
> *Erode it within seconds*

It didn't rhyme, it didn't sound like a spell, but it did the trick. The rock monster was surrounded by a tornado of wind and sand. The tornado got faster and faster, surrounding the monster. A loud whisteling noise sounded that caused the princesses to kneel on the ground and cover their ears. The monsters rock body was slowly diminishing inside the vortex of sand. When the monster was completely gone, the tornado collapsed in a pile of sand that blew away with a large gust of wind.

The sisters looked at each other and grinned.

"Thanks Autumn," Selena said as she came back to the group looking shaken, but unhurt. Selena opened up her mouth to say more but shrieked instead when the heavens opened and water came pouring down in a deluge.

"Sorry!" December yelled through the chaos. Her stress levels at seeing her sisters almost get killed had caused her powers to show up. "My fault." The seven sisters and Sir Kaill took off at a run towards the castle.

"Well done, everyone. Tomorrow we can start working together," Sir Kaill yelled over the thunder and lightning. "December, do you have any idea how to make it stop raining?"

❉ ❉ ❉ ❉ ❉

The last class that day was Faerie lessons. The girls were learning about what caused their disappearance.

"Seventeen years ago, on your parents wedding day, the dictator marched into our kingdom. He wreaked havoc for a full year before allowing your father to council with him. Your grandfather, the king, was ill, and therefore could not be consulted." The instructor paused and looked around at the seven princesses looks of extreme boredom.

"This is important guys. Listen up." The instructor was a woman in her mid-forties —or at least that's what she looked like— with her stringy brown hair piled in a haphazard bun on the top of her head. "During the meeting, your grandfather died, making your father king of Faerie. When your dad still refused to surrender the kingdom, the dictator's men shoved Emmaralda through the mortal portal—"

"Mortal portal," 'Tania interrupted, laughing. The teacher pursed her lips and sighed.

"Yes, the mortal portal, can we move on?"

"Yes."

"Good, now as I was saying, the dictator's men threw Emmaralda through the moral portal and left the room, leaving your father, Thíshién, and the dictator alone together. Your father was kneeling on the floor crying. He asked in despair why the dictator was doing this—"

"Do we have any other name for this dude other than The Dictator? It's not really specific and kinda lame." Milæyka interjected.

"No, nobody knows who he is. Whenever anyone saw him, he wore a cloak covering his face, gloves, and heavy boots. We're not even sure what species he was.

"Now, as I was saying, you father asked in desperation why the dictator was doing this and he replied and I quote 'Because... In 16 years the new century will begin and prophets have told of great stirrings happening that can only be stopped if your wife is here. I will rule the worlds and nothing can stop me. The mortal world is vast, and the portal never opens in the same spot in the mortal world twice. At the same time, the portal only stays open a year unless a royal person goes through. I doubt you will ever find your bride, and even if you do, you will have far more important things to worry about.'"

"So... the dictator knew about the prophecy?" 'Tania asked.

"Wait, is he the great evil... or does he want the great evil to destroy us so he can destroy the great evil and rule the world?" Selena asked.

"Yes he knew about the prophecy. We do not know what he meant by ruling the world. Selena, your second theory is probably more correct." The instructor paused.

"Any more questions? No? Good. Now we can move on to Royal Families and Marriage."

The sisters let out a collective groan.

"There are six kingdoms in Faerie other than this one, so seven total. Each son or daughter of the king inherits one kingdom. The first-born son inherits this kingdom and the rest inherit the others. Adopted sons and daughters must marry one of the blood heirs in order to obtain a kingdom. Unless, as in the case of Melody, the adopted heir is not a fairy, in which case the adopted heir becomes the king or queen of their species." The instructor paused. "Any questions?"

"Wait, so Caleb can only become king if he marries one of us?" Selena asked.

"Yes. Any more questions? No? Good. Knights of the royal castle must marry by the time their girlfriend is 18, and they must be engaged by the time the knight is 17. Children of knights are strongly encouraged to become knights, but it is not required. As Caleb is a knight, not only must he marry one of you to become king, but he also must announce which one of you he wishes to marry in three months' time. Time passes differently in the two worlds, so Caleb's age compared to yours is a little skewed. He is only a year older than you even though he was two when you were born. His friend Talon, your swords master, has two weeks to choose a bride or he has two choices. He can forfeit his title or allow the king to make the decision for him. This is risky business. Once a knight announces whom he will marry, he cannot go back on his word and the maiden cannot change her mind. It is courtesy for the knight to ask the maiden before he tells the king his decision—"

"May I see Milæyka?" Talon interrupted the teacher.

The other six princesses struggled to stifle their giggles as Milæyka got up and followed Talon out the door. The classroom the girls had faerie lessons in was a tiny room that could only be accessed from a door on the outside of the castle in between the outer wall and the castle moat.

"So, now you know about the pressure royal knights have," Talon said, extremely uncomfortable. He waited a few seconds looking everywhere but at Milæyka, seemingly out of character for him.

"I have some questions to ask you," he blurted out.

Milæyka looked up when a raindrop landed on her head. It had started sprinkling. "Talon—"

"Don't say anything yet," Talon cut her off. "Just answer my questions truthfully." Talon took a deep breath. "Do you think I'm cute?"

"What! Well, I... g-guess so." Milæyka stuttered.

"Do you like my attitude?" Talon asked, a little more confidence in his voice.

"Um... yeah" Milæyka said slowly. The rain was coming down more steadily now.

"Caleb said you seemed to notice me more than the other princesses. He said I should try you as my first choice. Especially if I liked you..." Talon trailed off and bowed his head. "Milæyka, I want to do something before I ask you my final question. Stand still and don't move... Humor me... please." Talon squinted a little in uncertainty and took one step closer to Milæyka. Talon put one of his hands in hers, and lifted her chin with the other, while biting his lip. Milæyka's heart started racing as Talon leaned closer and closer. An inch above her head he hesitated even more, then he closed the distance and kissed her.

Milæyka closed her eyes and wrapped her arms around Talon. The rain started pouring as Talon broke away and got down on one knee. "Milæyka," he said slowly and with great importance. "Will you marry me?" Milæyka's heart stuttered. When he had asked her out of the classroom she had had every intention of turning down the offer she knew he was going to make. But he really was cute and the kiss had been so amazing.

"Umm...uhh..." Milæyka took her hair and swept it behind her ear. "Yes," she whispered. Then she turned around and ran. She ran to her tower where she went out to the balcony in the pouring rain and looked out over the expanse of the castle. Talon was still standing where she had left him. "Yes," she whispered again. Then she turned and went back to her room. "What have I done?"

Chapter 8

_____Ready_____

The second sword lesson went only a little better than the previous one. Only two people got hurt instead of four. Milæyka was not there, claiming to be sick, so Talon paired with Bella. Selena and Caleb were still partners, which, once again proved to be a mistake. Selena still bore a grudge against Caleb and should have been kept away from him at all costs.

"*How?* How can you two manage to cut each other to the point of bleeding with *wooden* swords? I mean, come on! I expected bruises, not gashes…" Thíshién stood in the infirmary ranting at the two in question. "Selena, honey, why do you hate Caleb so? Caleb, why do you injure Selena so?" Thíshién looked into each of their eyes. "Work it out. You two will continue to be sword partners until you can make it without severely injuring each other!" And with that Thíshién stormed out of the infirmary and slammed the door shut.

"Selena…."

"I don't want to hear it, Caleb. It's over."

"Fine, when you want to know the truth you can use your telepathic ability to figure it out. I think these gashes are healed enough. I'll see you later."

After the door slammed behind Caleb, Selena looked around the infirmary, wondering if what Caleb said was true—could she pick a specific memory out of a person's head? She saw the nurse come out of her office and into the infirmary to care to a knight on the other side of the ward. Selena faced the nurse and concentrated.

Don't know what the king was thinking putting those two together as partners. It's perfectly clear to anyone else that Selena's suffering from a broken heart and that Caleb is the cause of it. I mean seriously!

Selena stopped listening, gave the nurse an annoyed look, and decided to try something else. She decided to go see Milæyka.

❋ ❋ ❋ ❋ ❋

"Hey, are you feeling better?" Selena asked as she opened the door to the tower. Milæyka was lying on her bed reading a book.

"What? Oh yeah. I just didn't feel like getting injured again. Heard you gave Caleb another piece of your mind," Milæyka said with a grin. Selena didn't respond and instead pretended to be studying the bed cover.

Selena concentrated again, this time on a question. *What happened with Talon last night?* Slowly Selena began to get a response. It was like watching a picture. It started all fuzzy, like a TV with bad reception. Then it cleared and an image came into focus. Talon was kissing Milæyka. Now he was on one knee and talking. Selena concentrated harder still. *"Will you marry me?"* *"Yes."* Selena looked up with a gasp.

"I can't believe you!"

"What! All I said was… Why are you looking at me like that?"

58

"I just saw what happened last night between you and Talon. The real reason you didn't come to sword practice today." Selena struggled to keep her voice fairly even.

Milæyka went pale and lay back down. "Don't tell anyone, please."

"Why not? They'll know this Friday anyway when Talon announces it in front of the entire kingdom."

If it was possible, Milæyka went even paler. "Well, what about you? You know Caleb's going to ask you within the next two months."

"Why would he ask me? He cheated on me." Selena turned away to conceal the look on her face.

"Well, he has to ask one of us so he can become king and everyone knows you're his favorite princess. Plus I heard he dumped that other chick." Color came back to Milæyka's face as the subject turned away from her.

"He dumped her?"

"Yeah, there's a rumor going around that he only kissed her because she asked him to before he dumped her. I think he made it up personally, but you never know. Maybe he realized that you're his true love so dumped her as soon as he got back in Faerie, maybe its just a cover up."

"You know what? If he does ask me, I'll read his mind and know the truth. In the meantime we should concentrate on training. The sooner we all pass the completion test, the sooner you can get away from Talon. For a month or two, anyway." With that final statement Selena closed the tower door and went back to her own tower.

Coward, she thought to herself. *If you really care about what happened between Caleb and that other girl you'd go read his mind right now.* But Selena knew she was afraid—afraid to know the truth in case Caleb really *didn't* like her. Guessing and knowing were different. If she was guessing, her heart could fall for him again over time. If she knew he didn't like her, she would never give him a second chance. And she really wanted to give him a second chance.

✳ ✳ ✳ ✳ ✳

By next Wednesday Selena and Caleb had grown so used to each others' fighting styles that all attempted injuries were blocked and they both came out of the lesson unscathed. By next Thursday, all seven princesses could not only use their powers, but they could use their powers to work together and defeat a group of ten highly trained knights including Talon and Caleb. On Friday, right before the engagement ceremony, the seven princesses were being fought by twelve knights—ten they had never seen before, plus Caleb and Talon.

"Selena, behind you!"

"Demy! Rock wall now!"

"December! Fire ring."

'Tania flew above the battlefield giving pointers to her sisters and shooting arrows with plunger ends at the knights. To keep injury at a minimum, each person wore a suit that kept track of how many injuries you had and where (though you weren't really injured, the suit kept you from getting actually hurt) and it had a sensor that told you whether you were dead or alive. If you were dead, you left the battlefield. The princesses had managed to "kill" three knights so far.

The knights fought with wooden swords. 'Tania shot an arrow at a knight attempting to sneak up on Autumn and his dead buzzer rang out. *Another one down!* 'Tania thought. December threw a fireball at one knight and "killed" him, while at the other end of the field Bella had a unicorn stabbing knights with its horn.

"Nice job Selena!" 'Tania called as Selena landed a deadly blow to a knight while invisible.

'Tania landed and engaged a particularly burly looking knight in combat with her wooden sword. "Take that!" she yelled as she stabbed him in the heart and his dead buzzer rang out. The sisters regrouped as the last four knights advanced. December encircled the knights in a circle of fire. Bella called upon birds to bring rocks and drop them on the knights' heads. Demy used the fallen rocks to create a wall around the knights while Autumn encouraged the fire to go ever higher and lick the sides of the rock wall. 'Tania flew above it all and shot arrows into the pit the sisters had created. Two buzzers rang out. The sisters demolished the pit to see who was left.

"Caleb and Talon!" December cried as the last two figures came into view.

Selena turned invisible and snuck up behind Talon, while Demy engaged him in front and 'Tania flew above his head. With three attackers, one of which was invisible, Talon's buzzer rang out in less than a minute of combat. Meanwhile the other princesses had Caleb pinned to the ground.

"Hey Selena, care to do the honors?" Milæyka asked.

Selena grinned and walked over to where Caleb lay on the ground. She raised her sword over her head and brought it down with a sharp thwack on Caleb's chest. The buzzer rang out and the seven princesses cheered.

"Yes, yes. The princesses won." Sir Kaill walked over from the sidelines. "Great job on the use of your powers. Talon, what did you think of their swordplay?"

"It was commendable. I think they are ready for their test." Talon smiled his smirk-like smile as he scanned the girls. "I'll mention it to the king today when I see him."

"That's right!" Sir Kaill yelled boisterously. "Today's the day you rope in a girl. How soon is the ceremony?"

"It's at five o'clock."

"Ach! We all better get movin'; we only have an hour 'till the ceremony. Class dismissed." Sir Kaill hurried off towards the stairs leading down from the rooftop.

"I wonder what his hurry is?" 'Tania commented as

they watched Sir Kaill sprint across the courtyard. "But he's right. I heard Thíshién say we had to be seated behind him on the balcony when Talon makes the announcement. We have to look nice and princessy." Everyone on the roof dispersed. As Milæyka walked toward her tower, Talon caught up with her.

"You looked really distressed last week. I know you can't change your answer even if you wanted to, but do you still want to marry me?" Talon swallowed loudly as he looked around, looking everywhere but at Milæyka.

Milæyka looked down at her feet then off at a distance before she looked at Talon and met his eyes. Her heart started beating faster and faster until she thought it was going to burst out of her chest. "I don't know," she whispered, looking at her feet again. "We're so young, I don't even really know you, and marriage just seems so final. I'd be a lot cooler about it if you phrased it differently."

"How about... Milæyka, will you be my girlfriend.... forever?"

Milæyka couldn't help it; she giggled. "Yes," she said, suddenly much more relaxed. "That sounds a lot less threatening."

"Okay." Talon swallowed again. "Oh I'm so nervous. I could throw up."

"I'm glad it's not just me," Milæyka said with a small nervous laugh. "I'd better go get dressed. I'll see you soon."

❋ ❋ ❋ ❋ ❋

"Thíshién, Sire, I don't think they're ready." Sir Kaill was anxious.

"Didn't they just knock out twelve well-trained knights?"

"Well...yes."

"Then they're ready, end of question."

"But Sire... The knights don't really want to hurt them, and they don't have any poison...The girls don't have their full powers yet...you know what happened last time...to..."

"I know!" Thíshién interrupted. He took a deep breath. "We have to take that chance. Things will carry on as planned."

※ ※ ※ ※ ※

'Tania stared in her closet at the array of gowns. *What should I wear?* she thought. She had narrowed down her search to two gowns: the one she had worn at her party two weeks ago and a similar one in a sky blue with white satin showing through the velvet skirts. It was quarter sleeved, so the sleeves ended at her elbow. There were pretty sky blue slippers that went with it. *I'll go with the sky blue one*, she thought.

'Tania put the gown on and went out onto her balcony. From there you could see the entire kingdom gathering outside the castle. 'Tania smiled and took flight. She would be at the castle balcony faster than any of her sisters if she flew. 'Tania laughed and let the wind carry her towards her destination.

When she arrived she saw two other sisters already seated: Milæyka and Selena. Milæyka was wearing a light purple gown with quarter sleeves and brilliant pictures of fantastic creatures embroidered in panels along the skirt. Selena was wearing an electric blue dress, also quarter sleeved. Her dress had four slits in the skirt showing off a lighter sky blue skirt underneath. The top was embroidered with vines that wrapped around Selena's waist and arms.

'Tania took her seat and looked around. The balcony was made of the same white stone as the rest of the castle, but this balcony had slits every few inches for archers' bows. There were pots at either end of the balcony that were filled with oil to pour on enemies. Just then, Thíshién entered with December, Autumn, Demy, Bella, Emmaralda, Melody, Caleb, and Talon trailing behind him.

"Okay. Are we all ready?" Thíshién stood in front of a podium with a microphone. "Ladies and gentlemen, we join together today to witness the engagement of Sir Talon Drakôn and some lucky lady. Before we hear that announcement, I have a couple of announcements to make. First, as some of you are aware, my wife has reappeared with our seven daughters. Please welcome Milæyka, Selena, Demy, 'Tania, December, Autumn, and Bella to our kingdom. They are sixteen years old, and in two days will take their training test. Second, I am pleased to announce that Emmaralda is again pregnant. In six months' time we will have another prince or princess in the kingdom."

"Pregnant!"

"What!"

"Six months?"

Emmaralda quickly shushed her daughters. "Yes. I'm pregnant. It's not that weird, I'm still in my thirties, after all. Faerie babies develop three months faster than humans. Now listen to your father."

"… Now without further ado, please welcome Sir Talon Drakôn." Thíshién sat down and Talon went to the podium.

"I hereby announce the engagement of me, Sir Talon Drakôn to…" Talon took a deep breath and let it out. *You can do this*, he thought. "Princess Milæyka Reye Analodan. The wedding is to take place in approximately two years' time when she turns 18. Thank you." Talon sat down. Everyone was staring at him and at Milæyka. Thíshién looked mildly surprised and Emmaralda looked a little shocked. But though they both were sitting frozen, neither was looking at Milæyka like she was an alien. Selena, the only one *not* surprised, stood up and went to the podium. "Thank you for coming. We will gather here again in three weeks when Caleb announces his engagement. Good night." Selena turned around to the stunned people sitting on the balcony. "Oh come on, people. Its not that surprising." Selena grabbed Milæyka's arm and dragged her into motion. "Let's go eat dinner."

Chapter 9

_____Knights_____

'Tania looked at her mom. "Are you kidding me?" she asked disbelievingly. "We have to complete that?"

"Everyone does. It's not deadly and it's really easy if you're know what your doing."

"Easy? I'll say. What isn't easy about an obstacle course?" 'Tania laughed as she looked out over the field at the course her teachers had set up. To make it through, the princesses had to ride their horses down to a brick wall, dismount, climb over the wall, and dodge between fireballs and water rockets to get to the monkey bars that were strung over a lake of orange soda. To complete the course they had to take a running leap and jump through a hoop four feet off the ground. All the princesses started at the same time, and the first princess through the hoop passed. The test would run for seven days.

The princesses mounted their horses and went to the starting line. They leaned forward on their horses' necks and waited with bated breath. The gun sounded.

"Go Skye!" 'Tania called. Skye took off at a canter, running neck and neck with the others. 'Tania reined Skye in as they reached the wall and laughed. *Easy*, she thought. 'Tania willed herself to fly and rose over the wall. She grinned as she flew over the fireballs and water rockets. Soaring through the monkey bars, 'Tania was twenty feet ahead of the others. Selena was running second, Demy third, and Milæyka fourth; the other princesses were still scaling the wall. 'Tania let out a cry of triumph as she zoomed through the ring and landed past the finish line. She turned around as Selena came through the ring. Her shorts were singed and her top was soaked. She took one look at 'Tania and smiled.

"I knew you'd win. You didn't have to go *through* the obstacles."

"Congratulations 'Tania! You may come back tomorrow to watch if you wish, but it is not essential," Sir Kaill said. "You can join Caleb in the library to plan your journey."

❋ ❋ ❋ ❋ ❋

"Hey good job on the test this morning Selena," Caleb said as 'Tania and Selena walked into the library.

"Why are we here again?" 'Tania asked sitting on the couch and picking up the bowl of chips on the coffee table.

"I'm supposed to let you guys help me plan the route we're going to take on our journey."

"So basically we watch you map it out." Selena summarized, also sitting on the couch.

"Yes, and I'm going to tell you why I picked the route." Caleb continued to tell them about the route while 'Tania leaned forward slightly to look at the map, and to grab the green can of soda next to the map.

On the map, 'Tania could see a huge island and a

round peninsula connected to what looked like a whole lot of desert. Caleb was pointing out his suggested route while 'Tania and Selena looked on from the sofa eating chips and drinking soda.

"Caleb?" 'Tania asked, interrupting his lecture on why they weren't going through the forest to the east. "Where exactly are we going?"

"Didn't I tell you that?"

"No."

"We are going here, to the end of Isle di Altri, the Island of Others." Caleb pointed to a spot on one end of the map on the island.

"The Ancient One's Lair." Selena read off the map. "That's descriptive."

"Its proper name is the Kingdom of Arcadia, or Arcadia for short."

"Where are we?" 'Tania asked.

"Here on Isle dei Fatati, the Island of Faerie. We live in the major kingdom, Kër Læil." Caleb pointed to the other end of map on the peninsula.

"Holy cow. How far is that?" Selena asked, putting down her chip bowl to lean forward and stare at the map.

"It will take us about three days to cross the sea and four days to cross the island. It's about two weeks from when we leave Faerie to when we get back."

"That looks a lot farther than a four days of walking..." 'Tania said disbelieving.

"It's really not that far; it's just a large map, three inches a mile."

"That's still a long way. Can we even walk that far?" Now it was Selena's turn to disbelieve Caleb.

"Yeah, of course. There's a marathon that runs in early summer where knights and peasants have to run there and back in two days." Caleb looked at 'Tania and Selena. "Why are you looking at me like that?" 'Tania and

Selena realized, too late, that their mouths were hanging open in shock.

"In our world, people don't do that," 'Tania stated.

"Really?"

'Tania and Selena both nodded, still looking at Caleb like he was crazy.

Caleb made an interesting noise that sounded like a cross between a snort and a non-committal grunt, and continued to drone on about the map. 'Tania rolled her eyes and zoned out, only to be yanked back into reality by the library door slamming.

'Tania, Selena, and Caleb looked up and saw Milæyka storming across the library, with Thíshién close behind her.

"Uh-oh," 'Tania commented as Milæyka came closer to reveal a long gash down her cheek.

"Milæyka," Selena said in a slightly whiny voice. "What now?"

Thíshién came forward and sat behind Caleb. He ran his hands over his face. "She got in a fight with a junior knight who asked her if she and Talon still went on dates even though they were betrothed. Milæyka blew up. I don't understand..." Thíshién trailed off as he looked at Milæyka. "If you don't like Talon... why did you say yes?"

Milæyka looked at her sisters and then at her feet. She seemed at a loss for words. "I was stupid." She whispered at last. "I'm 16. I shouldn't be engaged. I shouldn't have said yes."

Thíshién and Caleb's faces lit up with understanding. "You haven't done your homework lately... have you?" Thíshién asked.

"What's that got to do with anything?" Selena asked. Milæyka had looked up in confusion.

"After the announcement of the engagement between Princess Milæyka and Sir Drakôn, your history teacher assigned an assignment on marriage..." Thíshién looked

70

at Milæyka. "Did Talon kiss you? Before he asked you to marry him?"

Slowly Milæyka looked up. "Yes," Selena said quickly before Milæyka could figure out the question. "I read her mind. He kissed her first."

"Well... I have to go see to some squabble between two farmers. Caleb will tell you the rest." Thíshién stood and started walking out of the library as Caleb started the tale.

"Story time!" Caleb sang, sitting down. "A long time ago..." he began in a deep voice, "...when the marriage rule was first set, a group of rebellious boys challenged the king. They demanded to know how they were supposed to find their perfect match with such a limited time period, especially a time period during which mortals have been known to go through several girlfriends. The king was stumped. How could he fix this problem? The king went to a witch who sent a spell into the air to call upon the seventh prophet, the only one of God's messengers who remained upon the Earth. The prophet came to the witch and cast an enchantment over the world. When a guy kisses the girl he's meant to be with forever, he will feel a spark... a compulsion. He'll be compelled to ask her to marry him, and she will be compelled to say yes.

Thus, when a knight can't find a girl, the king gathers all the eligible girls and makes the knight kiss every single one until he finds the right one. Then the seventh prophet casts another spell. When a couple is married, a thin love enchantment is placed on them automatically that does nothing more than make the couple realize that the person they are now married to is their one true love."

Caleb's voice receded and a low roll of thunder could be heard as rain came pouring down, making a steady thrumming noise on the windows. Nobody moved as Caleb's words sank in. It was Caleb who spoke first. "You couldn't help but say yes—could you?" 'Tania and Selena understood this question to be aimed at Milæyka.

Milæyka nodded. Understanding flooded her face as she stared at Caleb.

"You should go to the infirmary and get that cut checked out, Milæyka," 'Tania said in a quiet voice as she too came out of the trance set by Caleb's words. She looked at Selena staring at Caleb. "Come on, I'll take you there." 'Tania grabbed Milæyka's hand and towed her out the door.

Caleb and Selena continued to stare at each other for a minute or two. Caleb broke the silence with a whisper, "Let's start over. You've never really met Caleb. You only knew Jake."

Selena continued to stare at Caleb, but some of the color was returning to her face and she started to blink.

Caleb held out his hand and whispered, "Hi, I'm Caleb, nice to meet you."

Selena stared at his hand, and then slowly, very slowly, she extended her hand. "Selena," she whispered.

Caleb's mouth lifted up in a slight smile as he shook Selena's hand up and down. "Nice to meet you," he repeated in a hushed, choked voice.

❊ ❊ ❊ ❊ ❊

The following days were fairly uneventful. Milæyka, Demy, Autumn, and Bella passed the test unscathed. The last testing day, when Bella passed, December fell into one of the fire pits and was seriously burned on the right side of her body. Causing the one event that made the following days only fairly uneventful instead of completely uneventful. As the nurse looked at December lying on the infirmary bed, she told the gathering crowd of royalty very clearly that December would live with minimal, if any scarring, but she wouldn't be fit for a journey for five weeks.

"She can finish the course after she's completely healed," the nurse concluded.

"That's cutting it close. That'll mean we can't leave until two weeks before the turn of the century," Caleb muttered so only 'Tania, Selena, and Thíshién heard him.

"It's fine," Thíshién said, his eyes rolling to the back of his head, his head shaking side to side—a sign usually meaning "no."

❈ ❈ ❈ ❈ ❈

Since December was injured and couldn't practice sword fighting or any similar activities, the siblings found themselves repeatedly traipsing to the infirmary and gathering around her bed for lessons in sewing and lessons in etiquette. 'Tania showed the instructor sample after sample of sewing stitches, each one turned down for simple errors. 'Tania and her sisters sat in the hard infirmary chairs for hours on end trying to please both instructors, for they had to perform proper etiquette while sewing their samples. Sitting up straight while conducting small talk was a trying task for young women so brilliant. 'Tania's only solace was that after each lesson, the sisters were allowed the rest of the day off. The sooner they produced an acceptable sample, the sooner they could do whatever they wanted.

'Tania spent her days flying over Kër Læil looking at all the wondrous creatures. Caleb stayed in the library making notes and maps for their journey. Milæyka could often be found wandering the gardens with Talon, getting to know him. These "dates" often ended with Milæyka and Talon in the sword arena dueling. 'Tania and Selena often joined them in their sparring matches, as did the others. All in all, the days passed by in a routine fashion.

73

The few days when the princesses did anything different were often spent arguing about whether this world or their own world was better. 'Tania found herself repeatedly seeking spots where she could be alone, in fear of lashing out at those around her. She still wasn't used to Faerie, and the stress it caused her to be away from the mortal world showed in everything she did. It was like being on an extended vacation, except 'Tania knew that this time, she'd never go home.

'Tania often stayed up late looking at the stars. She yelled at her mom and "dad" frequently about how inaccessible this world was, how frustrating, how medieval. She missed her three bookshelves of books. The faerie library didn't carry the same books that you could find in the mortal world. 'Tania had no computer, no mp3 player, and all of her friends were in the mortal world. Though she'd only ever had two. The cut-off from all she knew was getting to 'Tania. How could she ever get used to a world that was so completely different from the one she grew up in?

As December got better, however, 'Tania's thoughts turned once again towards preparing for their journey.

❋ ❋ ❋ ❋ ❋

A week later, December was allowed out of the infirmary bed for a couple minutes at a time. Thíshién had an important announcement. It was a week before Caleb was supposed to announce his bride and Caleb was becoming a nervous wreck. Though Selena was talking to him again, she was no closer to forgiving him and as a result tended to look frazzled, harried, or stiff whenever Caleb was nearby.

"Faerie life expectancy has been increased by ten years," Thíshién announced. "The marriage rule has

74

been increased by a year. Boys will announce their engagement on their 18th birthday and be married on the girls 19th birthday. That is all." Thíshién concluded his announcement and Caleb thanked his lucky stars. "How does that work?" 'Tania asked Caleb.

"Every time our lifespan is expanded, the marriage rule is extended. When it was first passed, boys announced their engagement on their 14th birthday." *Creepy*, 'Tania thought.

❋ ❋ ❋ ❋ ❋

The last three weeks passed with nothing interesting happening. Caleb's birthday was celebrated with a kingdom-wide holiday and lots of cake. Thíshién and Caleb became more and more nervous as the turn of the century came closer. Finally, roughly two weeks before the turn of the century, the nurse proclaimed December fit enough for travel.

"When are we leaving?" Selena asked Caleb, helping him store the practice swords.

"High noon tomorrow. I will be coming too, you know."

"I know... Thíshién thinks we need you with us. I'm surprised Mom's letting us go at all..." she trailed off.

"I think the prospect of losing her kingdom so soon after she returned scared her into agreeing," 'Tania said, as she too came into the sword shed to put away her sword. "I think she's also afraid of losing her new baby if there's another war. She almost lost us." She shrugged and left.

Selena looked at Caleb. For a second she stared into his eyes, lost in thought. This was the first time she had talked to him alone since that day in the library. She broke her gaze, suddenly embarrassed.

Caleb stared after her as she left the shed. "High noon tomorrow," he repeated.

Chapter 10

_____Starting a Journey_____

Black and blue clouds rippled across the sky as lightening flashed simultaneously with the booming thunderclaps. The Dictator looked up into the sky, at the maelstrom directly overhead. "The time has come," the messenger said in a low voice. "Spies reveal the princesses are to set out tomorrow. They will not return before the New Year. What's your plan of action?"

The Dictator held his pistol up and shot down the messenger with a bang. He stepped over the twitching body without giving it a second glance.

"MAN THE WHEEL! BRING HER AROUND STARBOARD! THE TIME HAS COME! TO SHORE, SAILORS!" the Dictator shouted over the thunder rolls. "We shall reach the Isle within the week," he said in a normal tone. He looked out onto the sea and let out a mirthless laugh. Somewhere, thousands of miles away, a princess woke up from a nightmare, then rolled over and fell back to sleep.

✳ ✳ ✳ ✳ ✳

'Tania woke with a start. She looked at her clock. *Shoot!* she thought as she skyrocketed out of bed. It was nine o'clock. She was supposed to start helping her sisters and Caleb get ready for their journey at eight-thirty. When Caleb had first told her this, she had laughed. When he had continued looking serious she had gone on, "Why do we have to get ready to leave three and a half hours before we're supposed to leave? You told us we couldn't take more than a backpack, and that's already packed. We each have one spare pair of clothes, water, food rations, and three special items. What more is there to do?" She had been mocked for her ignorance.

How was she supposed to know that there was a traditional ceremony in which all the travelers were presented with a couple items to help them on their journey? Normally it consisted of a weapon and a magical item.

Dressed in her travel clothes—a royal blue tunic with pink embroidery on the hem, royal blue pants with pink embroidery on the cuffs, a pink quarter-sleeved shirt, and a pink sash—'Tania ran down the circular staircase and ran into Selena, who was also hurrying. 'Tania smiled to herself, glad that she was not the only one who had slept late. She noticed that Selena was out of breath. "Ca-Caleb said th-that the ceremony st-starts in thr-three minutes," she said in between her pants. Selena doubled over for a second, catching her breath, then she straightened back up. 'Tania smiled even harder; there was something about Selena that made you cheerful. Together they set off again.

As they neared the courtyard, Milæyka, Demy, and Bella came into view. Demy turned around and started walking towards them. Her travel clothes were peach pink with a sky blue belt and sky blue embroidery on the cuffs of the pants and the hem of the tunic. A quarter-sleeved sky blue shirt completed the ensemble.

"It's just like our birthday party. Thíshién will call us up in order and give us our gifts. Caleb goes first." 'Tania felt a stab of annoyance when Demy said Caleb's name. She swore then and there if Selena was not Caleb's girl and he had to kiss every princess, she would punch him until he fell flat on his back and every bone in his body was broken. Caleb, who had known their dad— known him all his life and not told them immediately. 'Tania knew their mother felt the same resentment, but covered it well. 'Tania meanwhile turned to Selena. "Can you see what Thíshién is thinking?" *I want to know what's going on up there.*

'Tania watched as Selena's eyes went in and out of focus. *Weird*, she thought. 'Tania waited for a solid minute before looking back at Selena. Her chocolate-brown irises had rolled up, out of sight. *Creepy.* 'Tania shivered. As she watched, Selena came out of the trance and looked around for a while before focusing on 'Tania. "He was thinking about the journey. The first part will be on a boat. Remember from the maps? How this sea was more like a really large river running down Faerie, separating the Isle di Altri from the Isle dei Fatati? Well anyway, it's a pirate boat. We will all be given "identities" to travel under, so that we aren't recognized as the real princesses of Faerie..."

"How does that work?" 'Tania cut in. "There are seven kingdoms; how come we're the only princesses?"

"Apparently... all the kingdoms' young royal children are called either prince or princess, but when they marry, they become Lord or Lady. They have to marry another royal Faerie in order to get that title. Otherwise, they become peasants... We're the only real royal family... but if we all survive, and Caleb marries one of us, Melody will become the queen of her people, and each of us will get a kingdom. Caleb and his wife will get this one…" Selena's eyes slid out of focus for a minute.

"There was another prophecy, after the one about our powers that claimed a time when all of Faerie could be ruled by the true royal family, and would continue to be ruled by them forever." Selena stopped her explanation. "'Tania, we're stuck in Faerie… forever." Her eyes were slightly panicked. "What about our home, our lives, our school…"

'Tania's response was interrupted by Thíshién's voice traveling over the castle. "Ladies and gentlemen, today we send out a travel party to search for the Ancient One." He paused to let the applause die. "The first member of the party is Sir Caleb León Læil." 'Tania rolled her eyes when she heard Caleb's title. She had forgotten that he was a knight. She stopped her train of thought as Thíshién started again.

"He is going along as a guide and a protector, may your wishes be with him. To Caleb León, we give the compass of wisdom…" Thíshién stopped as more applause rang out, "…and this sword. It has the inscription of a wolf on it to remind him of his strength and cunning." The sword had a red tinge to it; it reminded 'Tania of blood. The wolf, standing on its hind legs, was engraved in a luminescent red that glowed, even in the sunlight. The hilt was a jet black; the only color came from three rubies: one on the bottom, and one on each hand guard. 'Tania couldn't help but stare at the sword in wonder. It seemed to capture her attention and suck her in. Caleb sheathed the sword. The sheath was also black with rubies forming patterns up and down the shape. 'Tania snapped back to attention. *Weird*, she thought, *a hypnotic sword*.

"He changed his mind!" Selena blurted out. 'Tania looked over at her with confusion.

80

"What are you talking about?"

"He's calling us all up and giving us our gifts in order... He thinks the ceremony will get boring and tedious if he doesn't..." Selena trailed off and 'Tania felt another stab of annoyance towards Thíshién and Caleb. She turned back to Selena.

"I didn't know you were listening to him."

"I wasn't... it was weird. I was listening to him talk and I heard him decide that... I suppose I was kinda thinking about what he was thinking, but I wasn't concentrating." 'Tania made a non-committal grunt, her brain whirring in concentration. She seemed to remember a conversation with someone—she couldn't remember who—that had something to do with learning powers. Something about the more you practiced the easier they were. She wondered if that's what Selena was experiencing. She had been concentrating on mind reading so much it was starting to become natural. *Like the alphabet*, she thought. *At some point you don't have to think about it to recite it.* Her thoughts were interrupted once again by Thíshién. He called them all up without— 'Tania noticed with amusement— last names. He only used their first and middle names.

"To Milæyka Reye, we give the stone of truth." Thíshién lowered his voice so only the princesses could hear. "It will turn red when someone is lying to you." The stone was bright blue and small enough to clasp your hand around it. Then Thíshién pulled out another sword. Milæyka's had a pink tinge to it and had an inscription of a luminescent pink butterfly, glowing even in the sunlight. The hilt was a bright yellow with light purple and pink amethysts set into it on the same spots as Caleb's hilt. Milæyka's eyes widened in surprise and awe as Thíshién presented the sword to her. "This sword is inscribed with a butterfly to symbolize her flighty and delicate nature." 'Tania noticed Milæyka's jaw harden when Thíshién mentioned delicate. She put her head down so no one would see her smile.

"To Selena Mirë, we give a telekinetic necklace." Thíshién lowered his voice once more. "While you are wearing it, you will have the power of telekinesis to aid your powers of telepathy and invisibility." The sword Thíshién pulled out of his bag was glowing a dark blue. It reminded 'Tania of the night sky. On the sword was the glowing blue inscription of a coyote. The hilt was pale yellow with dark blue sapphires. "The sword carries a coyote, which reminds one that though Selena's trust is hard to earn, when it is earned it is loyal until the end." Selena blushed when Thíshién handed her the sword and 'Tania saw Thíshién wink before turning back around. *I wonder what that's about…* 'Tania thought, missing the first part of Demy's introduction. She came back to attention when Thíshién lowered his voice.

"When you squeeze it, what you need will appear as an illusion. Helpful for getaways." 'Tania glimpsed a round leather ball before Demy shoved the gift into her pack. 'Tania wondered what on earth the thing was called. "The sword carries a dragon, a headstrong creature." The sword edges glowed peach, while the dragon was a luminescent peach figure. The hilt was a bright blue with some sort of peach stone set in. 'Tania had never seen a stone that color before and couldn't name it. Now that she thought of it, she didn't really know if the other swords had sapphires, rubies, or amethysts. She didn't even know if those stones existed in this world.

"To 'Tania Anne…" 'Tania looked up in surprise. Nobody had ever used her nickname in a ceremony before; she had always been Titania. "…We give a shield cloak." He lowered his voice. "It will repel arrows and most sword blows as well as allow you to blend in with your surroundings." As Thíshién handed 'Tania the cloak it switched from the gray of the stones to the royal blue of her dress.

"Cool," she muttered.

'Tania looked up at Thíshién and saw her sword. Her sword, glowing royal blue. *Wait a minute.* Looking at her sword, 'Tania realized what she had been missing. The swords were glowing the color of the their owner's tunics and the hilt was the color of their owner's belt. With another jolt, 'Tania realized that the color of the princesses' tunics matched the color of the princesses' bed curtains and the colors of the dresses the sisters had worn upon their arrival to Faerie. *Why didn't I notice that before?*

A piece of paper had been taped to the bottom of her sword, "Alternate Identity; Elizabeth Rush," she whispered to herself. *I wonder what we need an alternate identity for...*

"'Tania's sword carries a unicorn— a creature that shares all of 'Tania's traits." 'Tania, absorbed in wondering what traits a unicorn had, missed snippets of the next princesses' gifts. "...December... lot of thought... Morphing Jacket... Arctic Hare... Split Necklace... Griffin... Bella... Whistle... It will call any mythological animal... Kitten..." Then December and Demy were pulling her to her feet.

"The ceremony's over," Demy muttered. "It's time to go."

❀ ❀ ❀ ❀ ❀

The girls looked out over the edge of the boat. Caleb was at the helm. They were waving goodbye to all those who had seen them off. 'Tania spotted their mother in the front row. Her stomach was just beginning to bulge with the coming baby. 'Tania waved harder. "Goodbye," she whispered. The days coming would be rough going and dangerous, and 'Tania hoped with all her heart that they would make it back in time to save the kingdom.

Chapter 11

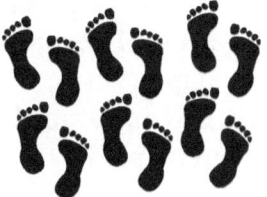

_____ Walking _____

'Tania looked out over the bow of the ship. This was their second day of sailing and small islands had started to appear. As she watched, a mermaid flipped out of the water, waved, and fell back down again. 'Tania smiled. It had been nice yesterday. She and her sisters had spent the day together while Caleb stood at the helm. It was just like old times, just the seven of them together. Selena had been more like herself than ever, and Milæyka had loosened up considerably. She felt happier too. It was like this was a vacation; there was no pressure to be a princess, no pressure to make a good impression. They could just be themselves.

'Tania spun around and skipped a couple steps before soaring up into the clouds laughing. She skimmed the water and saw the mermaids and dolphins swimming below the surface. The mermaids looked fairly human. The difference was the streak of color-changing hair, and the real mermaids— versus the land mermaids— had a slightly scaly look to them. Their skin shimmered under the water. She saw Selena and Milæyka watching her from the crows' nest. 'Tania soared up on the wind and hovered next to the cup-like basket.

"What's up?" she asked.

Selena looked over the edge and peered down at 'Tania's floating feet. "Do you ever get tired from flying?"

"Not really… it's effortless. It's more of a question of, 'Do I ever get tired *of* flying, which I don't… yet."

Milæyka squinted up at 'Tania as the boat turned and the sun went into her eyes. "I never noticed before… you talk a lot when you're happy."

'Tania pursed her lips and stuck her tongue out at her sister. Her reply was interrupted by Caleb's cry.

"LAND HO!"

As one, the sisters whipped their heads around in the direction of the islands. Emerging from the far off mist was a long beach; it must have stretched for a mile. On either side of the beach were tall cliffs shooting straight up in the air. To 'Tania it looked like there was no possible way to climb them. In the middle of the beach was a pier with a small queue of people and creatures. Then 'Tania noticed the other boats.

"It's a port!" she said, surprised. She flew down and connected with the ship deck while her sisters scrambled from where they had been. They circled Caleb and began asking him questions. He held up his hand and they ceased. "Here's what's going to happen. We have to declare who we are and why we are here. We will declare ourselves in three different groups according to the last name of your alternate identity. No one is to use their powers unless absolutely necessary. They will give you away. We are bound for the far side of the island on a sightseeing trip. If they ask, we are Fairies." He paused and looked around. "I believe the three last names are Turner, Rush, and Swan. The groups are three, two, and three." He moved to the base of the crows' nest. "If your last name is Rush, stand by me; if your last name is Turner, stay put; and if your last name is Swan, move to the right a bit." The sisters moved accordingly. 'Tania moved next to Caleb, realizing as she did so that this was the group of two. *Great*, she thought.

Milæyka, Selena, and Demy had stayed put. *They must be Turner*. December, Autumn, and Bella made up the Swan group.

"Why am I with you?" 'Tania asked, slightly annoyed.

"I guess the king thought we showed appropriate brother-sister dislike." Caleb said with a smirk.

Got that right, 'Tania thought. *I'm the only princess he's a jerk to.*

The group was on the beach now.

"Names." The guy was short and squat with green wrinkled skin and white hair coming out of his ears. 'Tania couldn't help but stare. She had seen a picture of the creature in one of her books. It was a knock goblin, the civilized cousins of normal goblins, who weren't civilized in any way.

Caleb elbowed her in the ribs. "Uhh… what…"

"Your name, miss?"

"Elizabeth… Elizabeth Rush"

"And you?"

"William Rush. My sister and I are headed toward the other side of the island for sightseeing." The knock goblin looked at Caleb.

"Why didn't you just sail around the island?" The knock goblin wore a suspicious glance.

Caleb looked stumped. "Elizabeth, do you still have those maps?"

'Tania looked up in surprise. "I think so…" She rummaged in her bag. "Yeah… here."

Caleb unrolled the map. "Ahh… That's right. This

map says that there are sharp rocks sticking up in the water to the right of the island, and a sea monster to the left. Whether that is right or not is in question. But that is why we decided to go through the island."

The knock goblin waved them through and turned to the next three princesses. "Names."

Milæyka stepped forward first. "Hannah Turner. These are my sisters—" she pointed to Selena. "Alexandra and" she pointed to Demy, "Charlotte. We are traveling with them," she pointed towards 'Tania and Caleb.

The knock goblin waved them through and turned to the last three. "Names."

"Carly Swan," December said.

"Morgan Swan," Autumn chimed.

"Sarah Swan," Bella finished. "We too are traveling with Will and Elizabeth."

The knock goblin rolled his eyes and then waved them through. 'Tania heard him mutter, "Why do Fairies always travel in large groups… It clogs up business." *Weird*, she thought. *We were the last ones in that line…*

❄ ❄ ❄ ❄ ❄

The forest beyond the beach was a redwood forest. The trunks were several feet in diameter and stretching more than fifty feet in the air. The still, misty air seemed to dampen sounds, the trees blocking out most sunlight so the forest floor was quiet and shadowy.

"It's so eerie," 'Tania whispered.

"Well, it's not called the Twilight Woods for nothing," Caleb whispered back. He had his sword out in front of him, lighting the ground.

"Caleb, how long is this island? You can't tell from the map." Selena was the first to voice the question everyone had been wondering.

"The island is as wide as your state of California."

Caleb had walked several feet before noticing that all the sisters had stopped with their mouths hanging open.

"You're *joking*," 'Tania said hoarsely.

"Would you like to look at the map again?" he asked.

He stooped next to a rock and pulled out the map and laid it on the rock. "See, we have to walk for twenty miles through this forest, then reach the first camp. Tomorrow we will walk fifteen miles through the Shattered Desert and three through the Purple Jungle before we reach the second camp. Then…"

"We get the point, Caleb—lots of walking. Let's go." 'Tania stood up and kept walking. Then she paused and turned around. "How many miles have we walked in this forest?"

"Six-ish."

'Tania grimaced and nodded. Why did they have to trek this island? She would have rather they'd sailed around the sharp rocks and docked at the other side. The wind whistled through the trees, bringing a chill. 'Tania reached into her pack and pulled out the cloak Thíshién had given her at the ceremony. She willed it to stay the same color as she pulled it on. Quite surprisingly, it worked. The cloak stayed the dark green of the pack. The cloak kept out the chill well; 'Tania stayed warm for the next several hours.

The princesses had started to drag. By Caleb's calculations they had walked about 15 miles. Nobody knew the time or how long they had been walking. "Can we take a break?" 'Tania pleaded.

"Sure," Caleb panted. "We need a break."

"What sorts of creatures live in these woods?" 'Tania asked.

"Almost all the goblin tribes are spread through the thousands of acres these woods cover. I hear this is also the home to the tribe of Woodlen Elves. They are like

Fairies except for their pointed ears and special magic—"

"Elves have magic?" Milæyka cut in.

"Yes… It is the reason they choose to live over here instead of on the island we live on. These are really more like continents than islands. Elven magic is difficult to understand. To our point of view, we see no connection to things they do; there is no pattern. It's not like a wizard who can do everything, or something you guys can do, which is limited to flying or telepathy. It confuses even the most learned Fairies. But I hear that Elves are supposed to be fairly friendly. We know that they have civilizations."

"You said something about goblins?" Autumn asked.

"Yes, most goblins live in these woods and dwarves have mines underneath it." Caleb drank some water and stood up. "We should keep moving."

The princesses stood up and moved after Caleb. 'Tania walked slightly behind them, studying the ground. It had become much more leafy all of a sudden. There were oak leaves and redwood leaves and pine needles strewn everywhere. It was like all the trees had suddenly dropped their leaves, but the trees overhead were still fully leaved. *How odd. I wonder if anyone else has noticed.* She looked at the others. Milæyka, Selena, and Autumn were talking randomly about some book they read. Bella was talking to Caleb about sword techniques and December was whistling.

"Hey… did anyone notice…" *Twang.*

"Ah! Nobody move!" Caleb's warning came too late.

Twang, twang, twang. The princesses and Caleb were hanging upside down by their ankles.

"What the…!"

"Why…"

"What's going on?"

"Quiet." Caleb's shout was loudest of all. "Listen," he said more quietly. "Do you hear that?"

A faint ringing noise followed by several hoots and yells could be heard in the distance. The sound was accompanying a stampeding noise. Caleb swung up and grabbed the rope around his ankle. His hand came away covered in green goo.

"Goblin spit," he murmured. "We're in a goblin trap!"

Chapter 12

_____Goblins_____

The goblins stank of rot and decay, their mottled brown skin stretched taut over their bones. Their teeth were like razors in their wide mouths and the horns on their heads were pointed to kill. 'Tania had never been more repulsed. These creatures were downright *ugly*. They tied the princesses to a really long log by their hands and feet and carried them off, chanting.

"Where are we going?" Bella asked.

"They're taking us to their fire pit. They're going to roast us and eat us," Caleb replied somberly, pulling against his bonds.

"EAT US?!" the princesses shouted in unison.

"Why would they eat us?" Milæyka asked in a hoarse scream.

"They're hungry," Caleb said, as if it was the simplest thing in the world.

"Why did they leave our weapons?" Selena was turning red from the blood rushing to her face. Her sword was dragging on the ground beneath her, still attached to her belt.

"To let us think that we could escape," he muttered.

"Can't we?" 'Tania asked. "I mean, we have super powers, can't we just get loose and flee?"

"No, we're in the middle of the goblin kingdom. There are goblins hidden in the trees watching us, in addition to those holding the log. They don't listen to our conversations because they don't matter to them. If we're planning escape, they won't notice, but if we try, they will kill us all." Caleb sounded despondent. "We'll be surrounded by a hundred thousand goblins. That's too many for us."

'Tania flew herself up to the branch she was tied to and sat upon it.

"There has to be a way to escape. Will this cloak cover two of us?" She motioned to her cloak on her back.

The sisters shook their heads. The cloak very clearly could only cover one person.

"How long do we have?" Autumn whispered.

"Once they reach the fire pit we have about an hour before the fire is large enough to actually consume us, but we will be unconscious from the heat long before that." Caleb too was whispering. Their death threats hanging over their heads.

"What about my Wishing Leather?" Demy asked, holding her leather ball out. "Could it help?"

Caleb looked at the ball like it was life itself. "It could create an illusion of what the goblins fear most and allow us to escape..." Caleb zoned out, thinking hard. 'Tania saw him screw up his eyes in concentration and wondered what he was thinking.

"Elves," he muttered. "Let it create an army of elves. Goblins are afraid of elves." He was talking louder now. The idea of living was revitalizing him. "'Tania, can you untie yourself?"

"Yes, but why me?"

"Because you can fly and you're much better at knots than the rest of us."

'Tania said nothing but did as he asked. She was internally glad that Caleb was not downplaying her and her sisters' powers and instead using them wisely. He was not nearly as ignorant and selfish as his attitude suggested. He really was becoming a better brother than she had originally thought. She untied herself and grabbed her sword.

"'Tania, cut our ropes. Demy, wish us up a legion of elven warriors. Everyone else, hang on to the log until the elves appear so the goblins aren't suspicious." Caleb took one hand off the log and took out his Compass of Wisdom. "We should run that way," he said, pointing in a general northeast direction. "Everybody ready?" he said as shapes began to shoot out of the round leather ball in Demy's hand.

'Tania waited for the shapes to make a formation of elven warriors, then dropped off the log and started to run. She came up short and looked back at the warriors high in the sky. "Elves have wings?" she asked.

"Didn't I tell you that?" Caleb replied from several feet ahead. He shrugged his shoulders and together the group ran in the midst of the elven warriors flying overhead. As the group entered the forest (they had been in a clearing at the time) they saw goblins running everywhere trying to outrun the elves. Caleb started stabbing those goblins that came to close to the group. 'Tania followed suit.

"How long do we have to escape?" she asked as she ran next to him.

"Only until they realize why the elves aren't shooting," he panted back as he stabbed yet another goblin. 'Tania nodded and fell back to join her sisters. They continued to stab goblins left and right.

"Does anyone else notice that the goblins are getting thicker in numbers?" Selena gasped, stabbing a particularly vicious goblin trying to climb her back. That seemed to occur to everyone else at the same moment and everyone stopped. They were surrounded by goblins, shrieking and hooting and waving swords in the air. The group backed up until they were back to back in a circle in the middle of the goblins. The elves overhead had disappeared.

"Make something else appear. Hurry!" Caleb yelled frantically. He swiped at a goblin that had ventured forward. "They won't hold back much longer."

"Why aren't they attacking?" 'Tania asked.

"They're waiting for their king to give the command to kill. They normally like to roast and eat people alive." Caleb's voice sounded dry.

Bella screamed. 'Tania looked around in time to stab the goblin that had crept up and scratched Bella. The ground was quickly turning red under the fallen girl. "Help!" 'Tania called to Caleb. Suddenly the goblins started shrieking all the louder. You couldn't hear anything else.

"Leave her!" Caleb shouted over the din. He was busy slashing at the group of goblins attacking him. 'Tania looked around. When the noise had increased, the goblins had attacked. All around her goblins lay dead and dying; her sisters were doing their best to kill as many goblins as possible.

"The only thing you can do is keep the goblins off her!" one of her sisters shouted as she plunged her sword into a goblin's back. 'Tania was too busy studying Bella to notice which one. Bella was barely conscious.

"Help kill goblins… Save yourself first… Or we'll all die." Bella closed her eyes, her breathing irregular. 'Tania felt tears in her eyes. She stood up and placed one foot on either side of her sister. Standing there, she shoved her sword into as many goblins as she could reach. She thought of movies she had seen, heroes making their final stand amidst a crowd of villains or creatures. They always survived. She didn't see how.

A goblin bit her leg almost down to the bone. She screamed as loud as she could. Her leg was on fire. She collapsed on one side of Bella. Kneeling there, she kept fighting. Out of the corners of her eyes she saw her sisters and Caleb being fought back towards her. She saw Selena go invisible five feet away. Goblins started dying in the middle of nowhere and 'Tania realized Selena was running in circles, killing any goblin near her. 'Tania couldn't help but laugh. It was comical in the midst of the battle to see goblins flying and dying from a sword stroke no one could see. Then she saw Selena reappear and crumple on the ground. Goblins were still dying from a tree branch held by no one. *If Selena's visible, what's killing the goblins invisibly?* 'Tania noticed Selena's hand clutched around something. *The telekinetic necklace!* 'Tania screamed in her head. Selena was still fighting with her mind.

Caleb shouted and leapt over to where Selena lay, killing goblins who got too close to her until he too fell down. It was hopeless now. 'Tania saw Milæyka favoring her left arm and Autumn standing over December, who had collapsed from exhaustion. Only then did 'Tania notice that the weather was cold and the air very still.

December's changing the weather! 'Tania thought. *She's so exhausted she can't control it.* 'Tania pulled her cloak on to keep from freezing. 'Tania tried to remember when they had last slept. It seemed like days and days ago. She tried to remember her mother, how long ago that last day was, when they had set off on this journey.

'Tania saw Demy trying to wish up another illusion while killing the goblins surrounding her and Milæyka. 'Tania heard a high-pitched whistle and was dimly aware of a new sound. She saw Milæyka finally collapse and heard wings overhead. The goblins were squealing now. They sounded terrified. *Thank you Demy*, 'Tania thought as she caught a glimpse of an elf. The whirring of wings got louder and 'Tania heard the swishes and thuds of several goblins getting pierced by arrows. *That's weird…the illusion before couldn't fire arrows.*

Her vision swam in and out of focus. She could hear goblins being killed and hoped her sisters were all right. Through her blurred vision, 'Tania saw thousands of elves— real elves. They were killing all the goblins. 'Tania stared at them. They looked remotely human except for their pointed ears and large gossamer wings folded on their backs. She noticed that their clothes were made of leaves and pine needles. One of elves came up to her and knelt down at her ankle. 'Tania's vision blacked out again.

When it returned, the elf was kneeling next to her, examining her deep wound. He touched 'Tania's leg near the cut, making her gasp, and then turned to Bella. 'Tania could briefly see other elves observing her sister's wounds. None of them had remained standing. 'Tania could see the elf by her was deeply troubled by Bella's wound. It was almost an inch deep and ran from her armpit to her waist. 'Tania could see the cut turning green before their eyes.

The elf stood up and walked up to a tough-looking elf standing some twenty yards away. They discussed something for a moment, then the first elf flew into the air and disappeared over the trees. 'Tania gasped as another wave of pain rocked her body. She looked at her leg. It was turning the same neon green as Bella's side. The pain was now shooting all the way up the left side of her body.

She fought to stay conscious while watching the goings-on around her. Her vision was starting to sway more frequently, never quite completely focusing. The tough-looking elf ordered other elves around the area.

Somehow the group had ended up fighting in a clearing. The trees formed a circle around the battle site.

As 'Tania watched, the elves cleared the dead goblins and tossed them into a cart. The elves wore little armor. Their pants were made of dark and light leaves forming a sort of camouflage pattern and their chests were bare except for the quiver of arrows and their bows. Yet they still managed to look fierce and opposing.

When the clearing was free of goblin bodies, the first elf returned. With him he had a dozen kinder-looking girl elves. They each moved towards a girl. Two went to each girl who had a green wound. The two by 'Tania looked identical. They had light brown hair and matching leaf dresses, and their eyes were a bright green. They knelt over her ankle and started discussing it rapidly.

"Goblin poison..."

"Very spread..."

"Needs to be removed..."

"How long do we have..."

"About ten minutes..."

"Surprised she still conscious..."

"Must be strong..."

One of the twins went to fetch a weird-looking elf with a large hairy mane and fangs. He knelt by her ankle and looked at it hungrily.

"What's happening?" 'Tania muttered. She didn't think they had heard her until the other twin knelt by her head.

"This is Ed. He is half werewolf and half elf. We keep him around for just this reason. He can withstand and digest goblin poison. He's going to suck the poison out of the wound so we can take care of it. It might hurt, but it will save your life." She stopped as 'Tania let out a gasp of pain. The were-thing had its mouth to her ankle, his teeth sunk in to her flesh. It hurt enough to knock her out again.

When 'Tania woke up, he was finished and the wound was no longer green. 'Tania noticed that her body didn't ache quite as much as it had. Looking down at her leg, she could see the bone in the center of the wound. 'Tania shuddered involuntarily and looked away quickly to avoid losing her lunch when she saw the blood gushing from her leg onto the ground. The were-thing was kneeling beside Caleb across the clearing. Caleb's face was twisted in horrible agony, his eyes bulged, and his mouth opened in a silent scream. 'Tania almost lost her meager lunch again thinking about how much it had hurt when the were-thing had knelt over her own leg. The pain had been exquisite.

Imagine one of your bones breaking. Then imagine all the bones in your body breaking. That is how it felt to get the poison sucked out. The twin elf girls were waving their hands over 'Tania's leg and muttering words in a different language. 'Tania looked back at them and then at her leg in fascination as the flesh slowly rebuilt itself and covered the wound. When the wound was almost healed, one of the sisters passed out, and the other looked up.

"That is all we can do," she said. "Some of your sisters are still unconscious. And the boy is giving us grief."

'Tania smiled at the thought of Caleb bossing the tough-looking elf around.

"We will take you back to our kingdom. You can fly with us. The others will be carried." She stood up and held out her hand. 'Tania took it and stood up. Her leg only twinged a little bit.

"My leg feels better," she said in surprise.

"Aye, we're elven healers," the girl said with a small laugh. "My name's Lizzie. I'll fly next to you and show you the way to the kingdom."

"How old are you?"

"I'm over a hundred." 'Tania gaped and Lizzie laughed again. "But equivalent to a 16 year old," she continued.

"Now come on. The others have left."

'Tania looked around and saw that they were the last ones in the clearing. She blushed, took Lizzie's hand, and took off into the now night sky.

Chapter 13

____The Elven Kingdom____

They reached the kingdom just as the sun rose over the horizon. 'Tania was momentarily blinded before she saw the stunning brilliance of the elves' kingdom. The sun reflected off of everything, shining its rays over the pretty scene. Waterfalls flowed over the surrounding mountains and flowed into a circular moat separating a large grassy field from the rest of the kingdom. The field reminded 'Tania of an outdoor amphitheater. Beautiful dwellings were built and chiseled out of the mountainside, and trees and flowers wound themselves over landforms and statues. Everywhere, you could see elves running back and forth, hurrying about their business.

"It's beautiful," 'Tania told Lizzie.

"It's home." Lizzie shrugged.

'Tania flew over to a waterfall and flew through it, laughing all the way. Lizzie smiled from her vantage point on the rock. "Spend the day however you please. I will come find you when everyone in your group is ready to leave." Lizzie flew up and soared down to a house. 'Tania flew through the waterfall again and landed on a rock. She scanned the scenery. Somewhere in the distance, a flute was playing a Celtic melody. She listened for a moment before soaring over to the majestic castle built into the rock. She had seen the elves carrying her sisters go this way. She landed and immediately saw the tough-looking elf that had been commanding in the clearing.

"Excuse me," she said, walking up. The elf looked at her like she was a disgusting rug. 'Tania tried not to react as she continued, "Where are my sisters?"

The elf sighed and rearranged his features to look resigned. "They are in the infirmary." When 'Tania continued looking blank he called a young elven boy over. "Show the princess to the infirmary," he commanded.

"You know who I am?" 'Tania asked with surprise.

"Indeed, Princess Titania. Elves know a lot about prophecies. We have always known the names of the princesses in the seventh prophecy. Now go see your sisters." With that the tough elf left, leaving her with the young boy.

"Come along, Miss Princess," he said in a high-pitched voice. He couldn't have been more than seven.

As 'Tania walked with him down the corridor she studied the walls. They seemed to be made out of a wood, but when she touched them they felt like stone. The young elf noticed her curiosity.

"Elves specialize in stone trees," he explained. "We use our magic to turn a pebble into a tree, then they cut it down and make buildings out of it."

"How does that work?" 'Tania asked. The boy shrugged. She supposed he was too young to know much about architecture. Then again, elves were longer lived than fairies; he could be fifty for all she knew. They reached a large oak door. Engraved upon it were vines and flowers around a large medical symbol. 'Tania didn't need the boy's words to figure out that this was the infirmary door. Her energy bubbling again, 'Tania burst through the door.

"Have you seen the kingdom, it's marvelous, it's spectacular, there are waterfalls and houses of rock and trees and flowers, oh there must be dozens! Roses and daffodils and lilies and all sorts of animals, I saw birds and deer and unicorns and…" 'Tania droned on and on about what she had seen in the kingdom.

Caleb leaned over to Selena and whispered, "I've never heard her talk so much… ever. Is she okay?"

Selena laughed and whispered back, "She's fine, she's just happy. She talks more when she's enjoying herself." They both watched 'Tania gesturing as she described the wonders outside. "But I have to say, I haven't seen her this happy in a long time…" Selena trailed off as she watched her sister.

She was floating closer to the ceiling every time she laughed. Selena started laughing too. Soon everyone was doubled over and laughing like maniacs. Even Caleb was laughing. That's how Lizzie found them when she walked in with the most beautiful elven girl Caleb had ever seen; her hair was a cinnamon brown and hung to her waist. When she moved it swung around her like a breeze. Her eyes were a bright green that reminded 'Tania of a pear, she wasn't sure why.

Lizzie looked around quizzically, assumed an understanding look, and walked over to 'Tania.

"Shhhhh…." she said, pulling 'Tania back to the floor. 'Tania stopped laughing. "As you all know, we have so kindly rescued you from the goblins, and we know who you are." Lizzie paused and scanned Bella, the only one still injured. "You will all be welcome in this kingdom until all of you have recovered completely and you have talked to the royal family." Lizzie paused again and walked back to where the pretty girl was standing. Caleb had his eyes on her like she was the world itself and Selena was looking at Caleb like he was a disease. 'Tania had to suppress a laugh at her expression. "This is Cassia," Lizzie continued. "She is the royal princess. She has a gift of healing and we hope she can help your sister." Almost as soon as she had said it, Bella let out another gasp of pain and her wound started turning green again. Cassia walked quickly over to the bed. 'Tania felt a pang of jealousy as she watched Cassia glide over the floor.

"Lizzie." she began in a singsong tone, "There's no need to wait for Bella. Show the others to the throne room; my brother is dying to see them."

❋ ❋ ❋ ❋ ❋

"I know you all are royal too, but please bow to the king and queen," the page said, opening the doors to let Lizzie, Caleb, and the princesses into the throne room.

"Princesses!" a woman exclaimed as she saw the group walk through the door. "'Tis an honor to have you here in our beloved castle."

"My Queen," Lizzie said, bowing low. The princesses followed suit, but Selena had to yank Caleb down by his shirt.

The queen waved Lizzie aside and walked up to each of the princesses in turn. "I am Queen Caia and this is my husband King Damir." The queen was a happy sort, bigger than the other elves 'Tania had seen, but smaller than her husband. She had sweeping black hair and the same bright green eyes as her daughter. The king was tall, almost six feet. He had long dark brown hair and a beard that went down to his waist. 'Tania decided he reminded her of the Roman god Neptune. She didn't notice the boy behind the thrones until the king addressed him.

"Dakar," 'Tania looked at the prince. He was handsome in his own right. His pointed ears and slanted eyebrows gave him a mischievous look. He had short black hair and eyes a slightly darker green than his mother's. She noticed his eyes were fixed in awe on the princesses. She tried to figure out who he was looking at. "Could you please show these lovely ladies to their chambers on the next level?" Dakar broke his gaze from whatever princess he had been admiring and looked at his father.

"The usual guest chambers?"

"Yes, and make sure they are comfortable before coming back." 'Tania could have sworn she saw Dakar blush momentarily as the king said this. She was immediately suspicious. She looked around again as Dakar caught someone's eyes. She noticed that Demy was blushing, but she wasn't looking at him. *I wonder if she likes him... he certainly seems to like her if I'm following his gaze correctly.*

"Wait," Queen Caia called. "Do join us at the gathering tonight; we would really appreciate it." Her eyes glinted mischievously as 'Tania left the chamber.

❄ ❄ ❄ ❄ ❄

Their chambers were interconnecting and resembled hotel rooms. 'Tania raised her eyebrows and turned to December. December just shrugged and rolled her eyes. 'Tania rolled her eyes too and stepped into her room. It had one queen-sized bed and a view of the closest waterfall. She heard Demy in the next room talking to someone and December discussing the journey ahead of them with Autumn. She sighed and sank into the bed. Before she knew it, Selena was shaking her awake.

"'Tania, come on! It's sunset; the elves are gathering in the middle of the kingdom." Through the open windows,

107

'Tania could hear the Celtic music she had heard earlier at a louder volume with more instruments. The castle around her was abuzz with all the people leaving.

"The queen dropped off new clothes to wear," Selena continued, picking up a gown lying on the desk. It was made of a dark green velvet-looking material. 'Tania had a sneaking suspicion it was some sort of woven moss. It was a simple gown with yellow ribbon wound down the front crossing several times on the bodice, going around the waist, and framing panels in the skirt. In each panel, a different flower was embroidered.

"They all match." It was only then that 'Tania noticed Selena's gown. Hers was indeed an almost exact replica of 'Tania's except for the flowers. Cassia poked her head in the door.

"Come on slowpokes, you'll miss out on all the fun." Smiling, 'Tania ran to the bathroom to change into the dress.

✳ ✳ ✳ ✳ ✳

The music was coming from a group of elves with flutes and drums. There were plenty of elves dancing what looked like a jig on the dance floor. Several of the elves were swirling around like they had too many pints of the frothing drink the bartender was passing out. Selena walked off to the edge of the dance floor and watched the dancers swirling by. 'Tania took a quick look around her and wove her way through to the bar.

"Do you have anything non-alcoholic with bubbles?" she asked. The bartender nodded and handed her what looked like a clear plastic can. 'Tania nodded and headed towards a bench by the edge of dance floor.

Popping open the can, she watched as she saw Demy whirl by in Dakar's arms. Smiling to herself, 'Tania took a sip of the mystery liquid. *Tastes like Sprite…* 'Tania thought as she watched her sister on the dance floor.

She saw a tall, tan elf ask Selena to dance and Selena's flushed cheeks as she said yes. 'Tania found herself nodding to the cheery music and tapping her foot to the beat. She swallowed badly. The drink seemed to get caught in her throat. Caleb hurried to 'Tania side and clapped her on the back until she stopped choking.

"Th-thanks!" 'Tania spluttered.

"No problem," Caleb muttered as he sat down next to her.

"Selena's really enjoying herself, isn't she..." Caleb trailed off the question hovering between them.

'Tania looked at Selena on the dance floor. They were doing something like a square dance and Selena was in the same square as Demy and Dakar. She had a huge smile on her face and she was laughing. Just looking at her having fun with Demy made 'Tania feel happy inside.

"Yeah... I'd forgotten how happy we all used to be." 'Tania continued with a list of traits in her head: *careless, fun-loving, confident... We were never serious if we could help it...* So much had changed since they had been in Faerie. 'Tania felt a moment of sadness remembering her old life.

Caleb broke her reverie with a sigh. She looked at him.

"What?"

"Nothing," Caleb said.

'Tania cast Caleb a suspicious glance.

"Would you like to dance?" An elven boy had come behind 'Tania. He had dark hair and a deep tan, 'Tania was momentarily lost in his deep brown eyes sparkling in the firelight.

"Sh-sure." She stuttered without breaking her gaze. She took his hand and followed him out onto the dance floor. The boy led her to a line of dancers and let go of her hand right next to her sister, Selena.

"Bryan," he murmured as he backed up into the line

109

going parallel to hers. 'Tania turned and shared a glance with Selena, whose own partner's name was Kile. The flute music picked up speed and soon 'Tania found herself whirling around in circles across the dance floor as she managed the dance steps in the complicated line dance. At one point the dancers formed a square and 'Tania danced briefly with Selena before twirling back around to her own partner. Breathless and gasping, she was glad when the song was over. 'Tania wound her way over to the bar again and asked for the same drink.

"Thanks," she panted. The musicians struck up a soft tune. *I didn't know elves had guitars... and is that a violin?* 'Tania thought to herself. It had a nice melody. She saw Selena on the dance floor looking around at the musicians, a faint smile playing on her lips. Demy and Dakar were slow-dancing on the side of the dance floor.

❋ ❋ ❋ ❋ ❋

Selena glanced around at the musicians. They had struck up a slow song. She smiled. It reminded her of her favorite song back home. She twirled around once.

"Whoa there," said a soft voice.

Selena had twirled right into Caleb's arms.

Caleb wordlessly took one of her hands in his and wrapped her other arm around her waist. He led her around in a circle. Selena's breath caught in her throat. She stared into his blue eyes. They were darker now that the sun was down and the firelight reflected in them like a spark that would never die. Selena's heart leapt. This was the closest she had been to Caleb since she had come to Faerie.

As they had started dancing, a singer had started singing. Selena lost herself in the words and in Caleb's eyes. She couldn't think. She could only feel. Her feelings were so apparent to her she was briefly surprised Caleb couldn't see them. But looking at him, looking at her, she was sure he could guess.

"Caleb," she whispered as the song ended.

"It's okay," he whispered back. He bowed and kissed her hand before backing into the crowd and disappearing. It was only then Selena realized that she and Caleb had not been alone. All the sound came back to her, suddenly too loud to bear.

She made her way out of the dance floor and up to a waterfall edge. She sat on the rock, thinking. It was not the dance that had troubled her. It was the fact that while she was dancing she had felt the love that she had squashed down into her conscience so long ago.

"It doesn't matter how hard I try," she whispered to her reflection. "I still love him."

Chapter 14

_____A Shattered Desert_____

Queen Caia and King Damir were sitting at the head of the table with Dakar and Cassia on either side of them. Demy, who was blushing furiously, was sitting next to Dakar. 'Tania steered Selena over and they sat next to Cassia. The breakfast consisted mostly of fruits. The only other thing was a wicker basket of biscuits. 'Tania helped herself to half a dozen strawberries and a biscuit while Selena took a biscuit and an apple. They ate in silence until the other four princesses and Caleb entered the room.

"Now that we are all here," King Damir said in a low wheezy voice, "I would like to announce that Cassia and Dakar shall be accompanying you to the end of the forest. It should take you all only a couple of hours." The king ended his speech and sat down.

✳ ✳ ✳ ✳ ✳

The forest again. It was just as before— dark, gloomy, shadows making shapes in your peripheral vision. 'Tania suppressed an involuntary shudder. Cassia looked at her oddly.

"Does the forest bother you?" she asked.

'Tania nodded, afraid that talking would give away the terror she felt.

Cassia muttered something about see-through leaves and 'Tania was suddenly warm with sunlight. It was as if the trees had disappeared and the sun was shining as bright as it could.

"Is this better?" Cassia asked kindly.

'Tania broke into a smile as she nodded. She could tell her sisters were also glad of the sun. "How did you do that?"

"An old elven magic trick," Dakar said, falling back from his position next to Caleb.

"Autumn can do it too," Cassia cut in.

"I can?" Autumn asked. Cassia nodded.

"You can do a lot of what we do," Cassia said.

"It is often useful in our goblin attacks since they dislike the sun," Dakar continued.

"Goblins don't like sunlight?" Demy asked.

"No, too much of it hurts their eyes," Cassia answered this time. 'Tania thought it weird that the siblings finished each other's conversations.

"How old are you two?" 'Tania asked wonderingly.

"I'm equivalent to a 17 year old." Dakar said in his I'm-bored-of-this-conversation voice.

"I'm like a 16 year old." Cassia said, shooting her brother a look.

He pretended not to notice and started whistling the same tune 'Tania had heard when she sat by the waterfall in the elven kingdom. Dakar skipped a step and landed beside Demy.

"We'll be at the edge of the forest soon," He said.

Cassia looked up and scanned the sky. "You should

be able to cross the Shattered Desert by nightfall if you don't get delayed. It will be much safer to rest in the Purple Jungle." She looked straight at Caleb. "Caution, the Shattered Desert is a simple name for such a poisonous place." It was odd to see such a serious expression on Cassia's face. Her cinnamon hair was swept in such an innocent way it was hard to take her seriously.

"Dakar?" Demy began. "What's in the Shattered Desert?"

Dakar shot a look at his sister before drawing a deep breath. "Well... the most prominent danger is the cracks in the desert floor that give it its name. If you're flying, the cracks make the desert look..."

"Shattered," 'Tania interrupted, "We got that part." Out of the corner of her eye, 'Tania saw Caleb smirk at her remark. She pursed her lips and shot him a look.

"Yes," Dakar replied, not noticing her look at Caleb. "The next danger is the windstorms that come out of nowhere."

"They are similar to what you call tornados," Caleb added.

"But they bring a chill that will freeze you as it passes," Cassia said, her voice grave.

"It's horrible, instead of picking you up..."

"It roots you to the spot and freezes you to death." Dakar finished Caleb's explanation. The sisters exchanged looks of horror. The idea of freezing to death in the middle of a desert was a thought that stunned them all to silence. December fingered the jacket she was wearing over her freshly washed travel outfit. She was lost in thought.

'Tania took a small breath. "Is that all?" she asked, her question aimed at Cassia.

"No... there are animals." Cassia said slowly.

"Animals... what kind of animals?" Selena spoke up for the first time since they had started out.

"They're called Volacocaries. A single one is a Volacocary." Cassia looked at her feet and didn't open her mouth to continue.

"They hide in the cracks and prey on unsuspecting people and animals. Their teeth and claws are poisonous… That's all we can say. The creatures are a goblin creation and are forbidden to be mentioned in the elven kingdom," Dakar said, his voice sharp. 'Tania looked at him in surprise. He didn't seem the type to ever get mad. After that, the group was silent. 'Tania started to fidget. It was too quiet. She wanted to hum, sing, do something to break the silence. Luckily it wasn't necessary.

"We're here," Cassia said. 'Tania looked in the direction Cassia was pointing. It was miserable. Nothing… Nothing but barren, sandy land broken here and there by black lines. It truly looked shattered. There was a line of life. On one side, trees grew and grass flourished. On the other side, there was nothing. It was so bleak, 'Tania thought that they would turn to skeletons as soon as they crossed the line.

Dakar was the first to speak. "Here," he said, handing Demy a whistle. "When you're ready to go home, blow into the whistle and Cassia and I will appear beside you." Demy blushed and pocketed the whistle.

"You're coming home with us?" 'Tania asked.

"Dakar is. I have to stay as crown princess, but I may visit you in time." She looked genuinely disappointed. "There is a river flowing down the right side of the island. It was recently created by a tsunami and has not yet been put on any maps… My parents have positioned a ship on the river mouth."

She bent down in the dirt and pulled out a map. She ran her fingers over it until she came to a place that appeared to be all jungle. "There." 'Tania leaned in. The spot Cassia was pointing to was about a mile from the

Ancient One's lair. 'Tania briefly wondered if the elves knew that that was where they were going. "The ship will carry you home." Cassia rolled up the map and handed it to Caleb. She waved goodbye and flew up into the air.

"That was brief," 'Tania commented.

She turned around. Dakar was saying goodbye to Demy. 'Tania was tactful and pretended not to hear.

"I'll see you soon," Dakar murmured. He leaned in and gave Demy a quick kiss. "Bye." Then he too flew up into the air and disappeared over the trees. Demy raised her hand and looked at the whistle. Taped to it was a small vial.

"Poison antidote," she read.

"Does anyone else think it's a bad omen that Dakar gave us poison antidote?" 'Tania asked with a skeptical expression.

"Only one way to find out," Caleb said and he stepped into the desert.

✳ ✳ ✳ ✳ ✳

Thíshién was pacing again. Emmaralda was due within a month, the kingdom could be under siege in eight days, and the elven kingdom had recently sent word that they had had to rescue the seven princesses and Caleb from a goblin attack. There had also been a p.s. It read:

They are probably about two days behind schedule.

The enormity of the situation was weighing down Thíshién's shoulders. He had no idea what to expect from the new century. To make matters worse, it was Christmas Eve. The kingdom called it Regaline Eve. Regaline was the day the kingdom celebrated the royal family. Everyone got gifts and the king blessed every family for the New Year.

But Emmaralda knew it as Christmas—a time for family to be together. And her seven daughters were thousands of miles away. Tomorrow would bring much sadness to the royal queen indeed.

❄ ❄ ❄ ❄ ❄

Water was scarce. The little bit of food they had brought was gone. The group walked across the desert in a near stupor. Nothing had crossed their path so far and they were sluggish and tired. It had been nearly five hours since they had trespassed into this forsaken land. The sun was high in the sky, baking the sand and those on it. 'Tania thought she understood why the only animals that lived here were in the cracks that littered the barren land. It was hard to fight the urge to go and hide in one until the sun had set. The wind picked up slightly as they continued walking. 'Tania picked up her water skin and drained the rest of the water in one gulp.

"December!" she whined. "Can't you make it rain?"

"I've tried! I think we're too far away from water for it to work!"

How can we keep going like this 'till sundown, she thought. *I don't think I can last much longer in this heat.* But as she stopped, she felt the air get colder around her. She sighed at the relief and looked to the sky to see why the sun had disappeared. What she saw made her scream. The others heard her and looked up too.

"Oh no!" Caleb murmured. "*Windstorm!*"

'Tania thought her heart would leap out of her chest with the fear that overwhelmed her. She tried to run and couldn't move her legs. *It's too late*, she thought desperately. *It's already taken hold, we can't move.* Though, as she turned that thought in her head she realized it wasn't entirely true. She could move her legs and her arms and every part of her body, but her feet felt like they were glued to the ground.

December knew she had to hurry; the storm was a few feet away. She pulled off her morphing jacket and wished that it was eight impermeable and impenetrable suits. As her new suit multiplied, she pulled it on. It covered every inch of skin from her head to her feet. She started throwing the suits to her sisters. The windstorm was now making a loud howling noise that threatened to burst her eardrums. She watched as the rest of her family struggled to put on their suits. She had no idea if they would work. Dakar had given no hint as to whether or not the storm could be conquered. Of course, he may not have known about her morphing jacket.

✽ ✽ ✽ ✽ ✽

'Tania pulled on her suit with haste. She knew where December was heading with it. She had suspected that her sister was planning something ever since Dakar had mentioned the storm. She didn't have long to wait. Almost as soon as she got the suit on she was overcome by a large swirling mass. She couldn't see anything. She felt pressure and probing against her suit. It was uncomfortable, but it wasn't cold. *Thank you, December!*

She sent up a silent thank you to December and contemplated her sister. She was smart and kind and always thought of others. She was always in the background, never rash or bold, content with letting others do the hard or challenging things to get attention. 'Tania had never paid a whole lot of attention to her sister before. There were so many of them... She made a silent promise to get to know all of her sisters just that much better. The pressure faded completely away and 'Tania realized that the noise had stopped. She opened her eyes to face the outcome of the storm.

Everything within twenty feet was icy and slick. Nothing of the sparse, scarce vegetation had survived. 'Tania slowly reached up and removed the hood of her suit. The air was cooler than it had been, but still really warm. As she stripped off the rest of her suit she looked at the silver lumps that had to be her family. She walked up to one and unzipped the hood. Caleb's face peered out at her, shocked but unharmed.

"Is the storm over?" he asked, moving his limbs one at a time to check for damage. 'Tania nodded and looked over at the nearest figure. It was slowly unzipping its hood. All of them were. Uninhibited joy ripped through 'Tania. Her family had survived the first danger of the Shattered Desert.

All of them seemed giddy. The act of surviving gave them a renewed strength they didn't know they had left in them. 'Tania felt like she could conquer several armies with her newfound strength.

The way before them suddenly looked inviting and opening. The group laughed and joked around, so nobody noticed the large crack until it was right in front of them.

"How large do you think it is?" Demy asked, trying to measure the gap with her fingers.

"I'd say four feet at least." Selena too was looking at the crack with interest.

"Do you think we should jump it?" Milæyka had gone over to peer into the edge. It looked too deep to go through.

"What about the monsters?" 'Tania asked. Her worry was barely concealed. She could tell by the looks on Selena and Demy's faces that they were thinking the same thing. Any monster that lived in a four-foot crack with poisonous teeth and claws should be avoided at all costs.

"We haven't seen any yet. Let's give it a try."

'Tania recognized the voice. She whipped around and

yelled, "No, Caleb!" but she was too late. Caleb had taken a running leap and was over the crack.

He turned around, "Se...*ahhhhh!*"

"*Caleb!*" Selena screamed.

A huge thing had shot out of the crack and had launched itself forward until it latched onto Caleb's leg and started dragging him back towards the crack. He had drawn his sword and was hacking at the creature's mouth with ferocity. The creature let go and croaked.

As it stood up, 'Tania got her first good look at a Volacocary. It was feathered and scaled at odd intervals. It was mostly a dark green except for several red target marks dotting its stomach and neck. The head resembled a dragon's head with neon green teeth and a purple tongue. The body was that of a vulture's, with dark black wings jutting from its sides. And the tail was... *a snake!*

'Tania screamed the last word in her head. The snake tail also had neon green teeth, a color 'Tania noticed that was also on the creature's claws. She remembered Dakar's words. *Its teeth and claws are poisonous.* This thing had two sets of teeth— one in its mouth and one on its tail. 'Tania's breath caught in her throat. She heard a scream. Selena had been thrown ten feet by the Volacocary.

That was enough to break 'Tania's trance. She took a deep breath and leapt over the crack with her sword in her hand. Her leap made another Volacocary leap out of the crack. She swiped at the thing's head viciously, all the while trying to avoid its claws and teeth. The thing made its first mistake. It leaned too far over its feet when it lunged and was off balance. 'Tania took the advantage and leapt for the Volacocary's head. Her sword clanged against the scales with a deafening bang. A thin cut appeared where the sword had struck.

The scales are too hard to pierce with a sword blade, 'Tania thought as she lept backward to avoid the monster's claws.

But the feathers aren't. 'Tania looked at the creature's chest. It was covered in feathers. I hope this thing has a heart, she prayed as she lunged one last time at the threatening animal.

❈ ❈ ❈ ❈ ❈

Milæyka leapt the gorge after 'Tania. She saw the second monster leap and go for 'Tania, but she seemed to have it under control. Selena and Caleb didn't. She made a split-second decision and charged the Volacocary that was trying to drag Caleb into the crack. She briefly noted that this one was much larger than the one 'Tania was fighting. A cold wind whipped around her and Milæyka looked up at the sky in panic.

"It's just me!" December yelled from her own battle with a Volacocary. "I can't help it!" Milæyka calmed down. The wind certainly seemed to make the monsters uncomfortable. Selena and Caleb both appeared to have a green wound. Dakar had been right. They did need the poison antidote.

"Demy! Treat the wounded!"

"I'm busy." While Milæyka had been fighting, she had missed the other two Volacocaries that had leapt out of the crack. Milæyka got a jab to the creature's leg and successfully managed to sever it. The creature took to the air. If there was anything more menacing than a Volacocary on the ground, it was a Volacocary in the air.

The one claw left could shred more easily and the tail could catch you unaware. Milæyka slashed and parried the creature's claws and mouth, but she missed the tail when it swung around. The snake teeth bit into her leg and she cried out. She was crippled now. She couldn't hold off this big beast. She saw flashes from the corner of her eye and was briefly aware of a loud thud some several feet off. She heard 'Tania's voice over the clanging of a blade on scales.

122

"Bella! Watch Caleb! Autumn! Help Selena! Demy! Help me fight this thing away from Milæyka! December! Cover us!" Milæyka heard a loud rumble and she was jerked backward. Autumn had used her split necklace to split open the ground and create a ditch separating the injured from the fighters. She heard Demy cursing that she couldn't use her power. Milæyka noticed with amusement that she was right. There were no rocks to manipulate. There was more clanging followed by several loud shrieks that sounded alien. Milæyka assumed this was the Volacocary. She opened her eyes in time to see Demy plunge her sword into the beast's stomach and 'Tania slash her sword through the creature's heart. 'Tania was flying. Milæyka shrieked when the Volacocary—frozen in death—landed on 'Tania.

'Tania felt the weight crumple on her. Knocked off balance, she couldn't stop the weight from collapsing her to the ground. What happened? 'Tania was suddenly aware of a seeping through her pants. *Blood*! she thought. *The Volacocary landed on top of me*. She maneuvered her hands up to press on the feathery hide. She pushed as hard as she could and felt the feathers give way a little. She pushed again, and this time she maneuvered her legs to help push as soon as the beast was far enough above them. The Volacocary slowly moved off of her. It moved faster once Demy started helping from the other side. The creature finally slid off of 'Tania and she gave a gasp of air. "Thanks for the help...Co-couldn't breath a whole lot under there," 'Tania coughed. "How is everyone?"

"Good," Demy said. "The poison antidote worked miracles. Even on Caleb. We practically had to bathe him in it though." Demy looked over at Caleb meaningfully.

He was the only one left on the ground. Milæyka had recovered the fastest since the poison hadn't had time to circulate all the way through her bloodstream. Selena was kneeling on the desert floor rationing out what was left of the food supplies. She winced every now and again, but other than that she seemed perfectly fine.

Then 'Tania looked up at the horizon line.

"We're almost there," 'Tania said, pointing to the hazy tree line in the distance. "A couple more hours at most and we'll be out of this desert."

"Thank goodness," Caleb said from his position on the ground, "I don't think we could do that again." The sisters looked at the tree line.

"What do you think lives in that forest?" Milæyka asked almost hesitantly.

"I don't know. But we won't find out by sitting here," 'Tania said. "Let's go." The sisters and Caleb gathered their supplies and set off towards the Purple Jungle.

Chapter 15

_____The Purple Jungle_____

The Purple Jungle was well named. When 'Tania woke up the next morning she couldn't believe her eyes. Last night the group had stumbled into a clear spot on the jungle floor and collapsed into sleep. None of them had noticed the stunning brilliance of the coloring around them. Everything was purple. In every shade imaginable. The trees, bushes, vines, bugs, and even the sky looked purple from down on the jungle floor. 'Tania just stared in amazement, moving to stand at the edge of the clearing where the trees began again.

"It's weird, isn't it?" Caleb too had awoken. He came to stand next to her. The clearing was a rough twenty feet in diameter.

"I didn't expect everything to be purple," 'Tania said in awe.

"Me neither," he said with a small snort of laughter.

'Tania rolled her eyes and refrained from asking why he found that funny. Instead she asked, "How long has it been since we set off?"

"I don't know… three days on the ship, one day in the forest, another day in the elven kingdom, another day in the Shattered Desert. So yesterday was December 25. Including today, we have six days until the new year."

"That should be a piece of cake," Demy said, also coming to the edge of the clearing.

"Well, if we have no difficulties, we can reach the Ancient One's lair the day after tomorrow," Caleb said.

"What if there are difficulties?" 'Tania asked warily.

"It depends what they are."

That's when they heard the scream.

The three jumped up and whipped around with their swords drawn.

"What *are* they?" Demy asked.

"They look like gorillas." 'Tania said.

"And they're taking your sisters!" Caleb shouted as he leapt after one in particular that seemed to be fighting with an invisible threat.

"How can they see Selena?" 'Tania asked as she hacked at a gorilla.

"Maybe she turned invisible after they grabbed her and they're smart enough not to let go," Demy said.

'Tania heard a shout and looked around. Caleb had been grabbed by a gorilla from behind.

"Demy, watch…"

"Ahh!" Demy screamed

"Out," 'Tania finished.

"'Tania! Fly above the trees to see where they take us! Don't let them catch you!" Selena yelled invisibly from some gorilla's arms. As 'Tania flew up above the trees, she got her first good look at the gorillas. They were purple, of course, with large purple spikes running down their backs. Other than that they didn't look any different from the gorillas 'Tania used to see in the zoo. Flying over the jungle, 'Tania realized her mistake. *I can't see through all this foliage!* She thought. 'Tania landed softly and looked around. There was a clear path of destruction where the gorillas went through.

"Well, here goes nothing," she said to herself. She pulled her shield cloak on, held her sword out in front of her, and started trekking down the path.

❋ ❋ ❋ ❋ ❋

Selena turned visible again when the gorilla threw her to the floor of a cage hanging in the middle of a huge clearing.

"It's like the goblin attack all over again," she said as she wrung her hair out. (December had made it rain while they were being carried away.)

"At least we're in a cage this time," Milæyka said with a shrug.

"I thought gorillas were herbivores," Demy said looking to Caleb.

"Don't look at me! I've never heard of purple gorillas before, and I don't think they're going to eat us," Caleb protested.

"Selena, where's 'Tania?" Autumn asked.

"She's on our trail. She's being cautious. She's about a mile away. Wait, there's a fork in the path. She doesn't know which one we followed." Selena looked up. "How can we show her the way?"

"See if you can get something to zoom along the path towards her," Caleb suggested.

"Using my necklace?"

Caleb nodded.

Selena concentrated. She picked a purple banana from the tree and tried to send it down towards the path. It was amusing to watch, if you weren't the one trying to do it. The banana looked like it was caught between two

127

invisible gorillas that both wanted it. The one who was facing the captives was winning. In this way, the banana found its way down to the path.

✱ ✱ ✱ ✱ ✱

'Tania started when she heard something. It was a small sound. *Maybe it's a baby gorilla*, she thought. She crouched by a tree and waited with her breath caught in her throat. *A banana!* She yelled in her head. She slowly got out of her crouch and crept towards the floating banana. She tried to touch it and it floated away back the way it came.

"Selena?" she said out loud. *She must be using her telekinetic necklace... Selena! Can you hear me! Tell everyone to try to drive away the gorillas so I can let you guys go. Have Caleb pick a direction to run!* 'Tania stopped her mental message and began to follow the banana.

✱ ✱ ✱ ✱ ✱

"Guys! Try to figure out how to get rid of the gorillas using your powers. 'Tania needs our help to get us out of here." Selena broke her concentration momentarily and she felt the banana fall to the ground. *Come on*, she thought. *Just a little bit further.* The banana picked itself back up again and continued leading 'Tania towards them. Behind her, Selena could hear the others discussing how best to chase the gorillas away.

"What about a purple leopard?" Demy suggested.

"We don't know if those exist," December pointed out. "What about a snow storm?"

"I don't think that would make them run away," Bella said. "I wonder if I could ask them to let us go..."

"I think they're all worth a try. Demy can also make

128

a rock monster to drive away the gorillas," Autumn said. The three princesses who could help—Bella, December, and Demy—stood up in a circle and faced away from each other. Bella tried first.

"Hey you! Mr. Gorilla!" The gorilla made a series of noises back. "Not going to work. They think I'm a sorceress come to steal their shiny things."

The princesses looked at each other and laughed. Spiny gorillas that collected shiny things— it was a weird concept.

"Are they going to eat us?" Caleb asked Bella, who relayed the question.

"Nope, they say they are going to imprison us here for eternity, or until somebody shows up who wants to trade us for more shiny things." Caleb buried his head in his hands and let out a moan of frustration. All of a sudden a cold wind picked up and snow started swirling around the cage.

"It's purple!" Selena yelled, dropping the banana again.

"Weird," Milæyka said, coming to stand at the edge of the cage. "It melts to purple water."

"Why is everything purple?" Demy complained.

Selena suppressed a laugh.

"Oh! Caleb, which way should we run when we get out of here?" Selena asked, remembering the last part of 'Tania's plea. Caleb looked at his compass.

"What's wrong?" Selena asked. Caleb's brow was furrowed.

"That way." Caleb was pointing towards a mountain they could barely see.

"December… is the snow thinning?" Milæyka asked. "We couldn't see that mountain a minute ago."

"I don't know. I haven't asked it to…" The wind was picking up. Soon it was howling in their ears. The gorillas below started huddling together. The sisters looked out of the cage at a whirling vortex.

"Ha!" Demy yelled. The others looked at her. "The monster is complete."

✳ ✳ ✳ ✳ ✳

'Tania pulled her cloak tighter as purple snowflakes wrapped themselves around her. Despite the sudden cold 'Tania had to laugh. It had been so long since the last snowfall she had seen. It didn't snow very often in San Francisco. 'Tania stuck her tongue out to catch a snowflake. *It tastes like grape juice*, she thought. What else was weird about this jungle? Then the snow was gone and a cold wind came up.

This is way less fun, 'Tania thought as she had to pull her cloak even tighter. Loud gorilla shrieks pierced the air. Purple spiked bodies could be seen running in every direction. *What's going on?* Then she saw the monster. *Oh my gosh Demy! Couldn't you have made that thing smaller?* 'Tania shouted in her head as she had to dive aside to avoid being squashed. The monster was at least three times the size of the one Demy had accidentally created while she was practicing, and it was purple. *Where'd the banana go?* 'Tania took off running in the direction that the gorillas were coming from.

✳ ✳ ✳ ✳ ✳

It had been several hours since the group had been stuck in the cage and it was beginning to get cramped. They were sore from being carried by gorillas for two hours and bad-tempered from being in the cage for the next three hours. The gorillas had been running off for about an hour now as the rock monster crushed and pounded the forest around them.

130

"Where's 'Tania?" Demy asked.

"Still fighting her way through the gorillas. They seem to be evacuating 360 degrees. 'Tania can't find a straight path and has to keep zig-zagging to avoid your monster." Selena replied after searching 'Tania's thoughts for her location.

"I have an idea," Demy said. "Hey Monster! Find 'Tania and bring her here!" The monster grunted and moved off. "Did it work?"

They heard 'Tania scream in the distance.

"It worked," Selena said. "You know she could have flown over to us and avoided the gorillas altogether."

"She was probably afraid the rock monster would hit her and make her fall," Milæyka said, standing up stiffly.

"Here she is!" December shouted over the grinding of the returning monster.

❄ ❄ ❄ ❄ ❄

Demy! Tell your monster to put me down! 'Tania yelled in her head to no effect. Selena wasn't transferring her message. As the monster entered the clearing, 'Tania saw Autumn hunkered down in a corner of the cage with a look of intense concentration on her face. Milæyka, Selena, and Demy were at the bars waiting for her.

"Rock! Let go!" Demy yelled.

'Tania had to catch herself as the monster dropped her into open air. "Thanks," she said sarcastically to Demy who shrugged in answer. "Where's the latch?"

"On top. The top will lift off and we can jump to the ground." (Which was ten feet away.)

"Gotcha." As 'Tania flew up to the latch she could hear Caleb talking to Selena right below her.

"You really are amazing, you know," Caleb said softly.

'Tania could almost see the blood rising to Selena's face as she blushed.

131

"Which way does your compass point?" she asked, changing the subject. Caleb pointed at Selena.

"What?!" Selena practically screamed.

Not smooth, dude, 'Tania thought form her vantage point.

"I meant we have to run in the direction that your back is facing," Caleb amended.

"Got it!" 'Tania called. She grabbed the handle and pulled with all her strength until it popped free. The group leapt out of the cage, except for Autumn.

"Autumn, come on," 'Tania said. Autumn was mumbling a bunch of nonsense words. "What's wrong with her?" 'Tania asked.

The sisters shrugged. Autumn's chanting got louder.

"Bomen van oud die vóór me komen ga ik een gunst van thee vragen wij rechte passage aan wat daarna komt nodig hebben en u geven ons enkel dat nodig."

There was a loud ripping noise and all the trees in the direction Caleb had pointed uprooted and moved somewhere else creating a passage through the trees similar to a hallway.

"Cool," Demy said.

"Uhh… Guys, we have company," Selena said, only slightly hysterical. The gorillas were back and they were attacking the rock monster with spears.

"What do we do?" 'Tania asked quietly.

"Run for the passage as fast as we can and hope they don't notice?" Milæyka suggested.

"That's alright with me," Caleb said.

"Run!" Demy screamed as the rock monster's arm fell off.

'Tania took off flying down the path.

"I think it's working!" Selena yelled.

Then the gorillas started shrieking again.

"Never mind! Run faster!" Selena amended.

A spear landed next to Milæyka's heel and she yelled. The leading gorilla grabbed December and she fell.

"December!"

Autumn stopped and jammed her sword into the gorilla's arm. December got up and kept running. The spears were getting closer. At a full sprint, the group was covering three times as much ground as they would have if they were walking. 'Tania was flying at the back of the group, fighting off the gorillas that got too close. The group got within one hundred feet of the end of the purple; they could see green up ahead.

"They're falling back! Keep going!" 'Tania yelled as she hit the ground and kept running. They were soon engulfed in the sea of green they had seen. They slowed to a walk. "Where are we?" 'Tania asked.

"I don't know," Selena said, walking forward a little more.

There was a sudden intake and a grinding of metal as a cage erupted out of the ground and shot into the air, taking the princesses and Caleb with it.

"Not again!" Demy and Selena moaned simultaneously.

"We're in the Plains of Ramin," Caleb answered.

Chapter 16

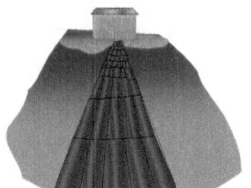

_____Calder & Callix_____

The cage was noticeably smaller than the last one. It was amazing that all of the sisters and Caleb had managed to fit on the floor. "What do you think owns these cages?" 'Tania asked Caleb.

"I don't know, but whatever it is probably trying to catch gorillas that come out of the forest."

"Do you think they're human?" Milæyka asked.

"If by human you mean fairies, elves, or dwarves, then yes. These traps are too well made to be some goblin invention." He said, running his hands down the smooth bars that imprisoned the sisters.

"I don't remember planning to go through the Plains of Ramin," Selena said with a slight question in her voice.

Caleb sighed. "We're not. Going through the Plains of Ramin takes us a day or two out of our way. It's also an uncharted territory—no one who comes in goes out. Nobody knows what lives here; they only know that it is an unforgiving land. We also have to go up the mountain from the other side, which is steeper and more perilous.

We'll have to take it slowly to ensure we don't fall off." This was the worst news. Especially since the sun was going down...again.

"Do the days seem shorter to you guys?" 'Tania asked.

"It is winter. There are only six to eight hours of sunlight a day," Caleb said.

"But it's so warm out. It feels like we're on the equator and the days don't get shorter there," Demy pointed out.

"It's warm because of all the magic that flows through here. You only ever get warm weather here. Unless someone like December decides to make it snow." December blushed. "Trust me. We only have like six hours of sunlight a day. That's why it always seems like the sun's setting."

"How long do you think we'll be in this cage?" 'Tania asked.

"Not long at all by my reckoning," said a voice from outside the cage. "Let'm down Calder."

There was a loud grinding noise as the cage was lowered from its position ten feet in the air. The cage walls lowered and the princesses tumbled out of the cage. The boy who had spoken leaned down and held out his hand for 'Tania.

"Thanks," she muttered.

He smiled. "I'm Callix and this is my buddy Calder." Callix had dark brown hair, like Selena's, and dark blue eyes. 'Tania felt her heart stutter as Callix smiled again. He looked a lot like Caleb in some ways, 'Tania realized when Caleb, who had helped Selena up, came and stood next to him. Calder helped Autumn up then came to stand beside Caleb and Callix. Calder had longer chestnut hair and deep green eyes. If he had had pointy ears, 'Tania would have called him an elf in a heartbeat. But both guys looked normal.

"Who are you guys?" Demy asked.

"He just told you. I'm Calder and he's Callix," Calder said with a slight exasperation.

"No, I mean, why are you here and why were we in a cage?" Demy corrected.

"We're the Raminian people. We eat the gorillas that sometimes get caught in these cages," Callix said.

"Who are the Raminian people?" 'Tania asked.

"The Lost People, The Wanderers...Any of this familiar?" Calder asked.

"No." Selena said frankly.

"These lands are classified as uncharted; nobody knows what's here," Caleb said slowly.

Caleb and Callix exchanged an exasperated look.

"We live here in a civilization of lost explorers and their kin. Most people who come this way fall in love with the lifestyle or can't figure a way out," Callix explained.

"We were both found wandering around out here on our own. I was three," Calder said.

"I was seven," Callix added.

"How old are you now?" Autumn asked.

"Sixteen," they said at the same time.

'Tania noticed that Milæyka was holding her Stone of Truth behind her back. It was still blue.

"Come with us. We can give you places to sleep for the night in our village," Calder continued.

"That would be great," Caleb said.

"Cool. The village is about a mile from here." Callix started walking away.

"What are your names?" Calder asked.

Caleb was first to answer. "William. Will actually." So Caleb still didn't trust them.

"I'm his sister Elizabeth," 'Tania said, catching up to Callix at the front.

Selena was the next to speak. "We're their friends. I'm Alex. And that's my sister Hannah," she pointed at Milæyka, "and that's my other sister Charlotte." She pointed at Demy.

"I'm Sarah," Bella said. "Sarah Swan."

"I'm Morgan," Autumn told Calder. "Sarah's sister. And that's our other sister Carly." Autumn pointed at December, who looked like she hadn't been able to remember her alter ego.

'Tania smiled. It had taken her a moment or two before she could remember her name.

"Where are you all headed?" Callix asked.

"Up the mountain," 'Tania replied. "We came to explore the island. We're going back home soon though. There's a ship waiting for us at the entrance to the river."

"I know that ship," Callix said with a small wink. "It's an elven trade ship. You guys gonna hitch a ride back to Faerie on it?"

'Tania smiled back at him. "Yeah. Yeah we are."

"I wouldn't mind going back to Faerie," Calder said softly.

"Me neither Calder, me neither," said Callix.

"Why do you guys live out here if you don't want to?" 'Tania asked.

"We came from Faerie. We were kidnapped—Calder at an age too young to remember much. Me," Callix snorted slightly. "I remember that my dad had power. We lived in a large house. A group of rebels kidnapped me for ransom, but had no intention of returning me. So I ran away. Calder and his foster father found me in a cage like the one we just let you out of. I do remember that my dad was really protective of me because I was his last son. I was a triplet.

One was accidentally left behind at a picnic area we were only a few months old. I remember my dad being really upset about that one. My mom died trying to find him again. There was a rumor that she found him as she

138

was dying and gave him to a passing knight to take care of...the other one was stolen at two and a half years of age." Callix trailed off. "That's all I remember of my past. I don't even know if that's true." He lapsed into silence.

'Tania looked at Caleb who was walking in stony silence. Selena was walking beside, him her hand hovering near his. 'Tania realized that Selena longed to comfort Caleb—he looked visibly distressed. 'Tania wondered why, but her thoughts were interrupted by Calder, who started talking.

"We're here," he said, pulling back the grass. "Welcome to the village of Ramin."

'Tania was taken aback. In front of her was a pond. There was a complicated dock running over it with lights making the water sparkle. The houses on the pond's edge were made of mud and seemed to have grass thatched on the roof. It was simple, but beautiful.

"Wow," she said.

Callix smiled and held out his hand. "Come on. I'll show you the guest hut." 'Tania smiled back and hoped Callix couldn't see the blush forming on her cheeks. She took his hand slowly.

"'Kay," she said.

The guest hut was the farthest from the edge of the pond they had entered on. On the inside it had several thatched mattresses, some blankets in a corner, and a small kitchen on one wall.

"The bathrooms out back. The shower is through that door." Calder pointed towards a door that 'Tania had failed to notice. "Tell somebody tomorrow if the mechanics in the bathroom aren't working properly."

"Goodnight," Callix said and he ducked out of the door, taking Calder with him.

"So...who wants to shower first?"

Oh to be clean. 'Tania had forgotten how nice it was

to be clean. Callix had come back soon after with food and drinks. It had been a great meal. 'Tania hadn't eaten well since they had left the elven kingdom.

That was also the last time she had been clean and though it had only been two days, 'Tania had blood on her where the Volacocary had landed and she smelled like a gorilla. She had a large bruise around her midsection where the rock monster had grabbed her and more where she had whacked herself on the cage. All the sisters were sore and achy, but it was with a full stomach and clean bodies that they lay down to rest.

※ ※ ※ ※ ※

"Everybody up! I have breakfast," Callix called in the morning.

"What time is it?" Milæyka moaned.

"Nine, according to the sun dial in the middle of the pond," Calder replied. He had a low table with him that he set in the middle of the makeshift beds.

Callix sat down on the end of 'Tania's bed and started spreading out the food. 'Tania propped herself up by her elbows.

"That smells good," she said.

"Homemade breads and biscuits and some homegrown jellies. Plus some fruit from my foster mother's garden," Callix boasted. 'Tania sat up the rest of the way and picked up a biscuit sitting on top.

"These are really good," she said. Soon everyone was talking and laughing and eating the food.

"You guys have, like, your very own society out here," Demy said as she helped herself to another biscuit with grape jelly.

"Yeah. It is said to have been set up a long time ago by the one of the first Faerie explorers. Their ship got

140

dashed on the rocks and they founded a colony. When they were finally found, half of them decided to stay." Calder shrugged like it was a huge myth.

"We don't have many conveniences though," Calder said with a grimace. "Outdoor bathrooms and several of us don't even have running water. Sometimes we feel like we're living in the dark ages."

Autumn grimaced too.

"You know... You could always come back with us," 'Tania said cautiously.

Callix looked at her like she was an angel.

"You would seriously take us with you?" Calder asked.

"Yeah, sure. You guys can train to become knights." 'Tania snuck a glance at Caleb. His face was stony. "Ca-Will is a knight. Aren't you, Will?" 'Tania blushed. She had almost forgotten that they were undercover.

"Uh... yeah. I am. Hey Elizabeth, Alex, can I speak to you guys alone for a moment?" He stood up and left.

"What's up with him?" Calder asked.

'Tania shrugged. When she got up to follow Caleb out the door, she realized she had been holding Callix's hand. 'Tania blushed and hurried through the door with Selena right behind her.

"Caleb! What is your problem?" 'Tania demanded as soon as she came out of the door.

"I don't think we can trust these guys," he said.

"I watched Milæyka's truth stone yesterday. Everything they said was true. Or at least they *thought* it was true," 'Tania said.

"I still don't think they're trustworthy." Caleb said stubbornly.

"Milæyka!" Selena called. "We need you."

"Yeah?" Milæyka appeared at the door a second later.

"Make him tell us why he doesn't like Callix

and Calder," Selena requested with a hint of her old mischievous tone of voice. Milæyka smiled.

"With pleasure," Milæyka closed her eyes and brought one arm towards her face. Her brow furrowed and her body seemed to ripple before she opened her eyes and snapped. The snap seemed to ring around the pond and hang in the air. Caleb jerked slightly.

"Caleb? Why do you not trust the guys in there?" Milæyka asked calmly.

"Don't mistrust... Am scared." Caleb seemed to be having trouble talking.

"He's resisting," Milæyka said, "Caleb, why are you upset?"

"Guys in there. Might be my brothers. Old story. Father dead. Mother dead. Knight dead. Captors found in goblin cage. Boys never found. Lord died. Guys royal."

"Did that make sense to either of you?" Milæyka asked.

"I think he's talking about the story Callix told us last night, about his childhood in Faerie. He said he was a triplet and his other brothers were missing. Caleb said something about the guys in there being his brothers. You don't think he's the baby left on the picnic, do you? He did mutter something about a knight dead and mother dead." 'Tania started babbling as it made less and less sense.

Milæyka snapped her fingers again and Caleb came out of the trance he was in.

"Caleb... Do you think Callix and Calder are your brothers?"

"Yes," Caleb said.

"Then why do you keep saying we can't trust them?" 'Tania exploded.

"Because I'm the youngest. That's the story. The youngest triplet got lost first. If they come back to Faerie I will never be king of Kër Læil," Caleb ranted.

142

"What's Kër Læil again?" Selena asked.

"Your father's kingdom. As the only boy, I inherit the kingdom when I marry one of you. The other six princesses get the other surrounding kingdoms that are currently ruled by lords and ladies. I was a meager Lord's son until your uncle adopted me, then I was readopted by your father. Now because of them I can't be king of my kingdom." Caleb was really upset.

Selena walked over to where he sat at the water's edge and grabbed his hand. "Hey," she said gently wiping hair out of his eyes. "You just said it yourself. *You* were adopted by the king. They weren't. They won't be. *You* are the heir to the throne of Kër Læil if you marry a princess. *They* will be stuck with whatever kingdom their princess marries, or a common house if they don't marry one of us. There are seven kingdoms. There are seven princesses and *one* adopted son." Selena paused and looked up at 'Tania.

"She's right, Caleb," 'Tania agreed. "You were adopted by the king; they weren't. Only you can become king of Kër Læil."

Caleb looked up at them and smiled. "You're right. Thanks." He stood up and hugged Selena before going back into the hut. Selena looked like she had stopped breathing.

"Selena. Breathe!" 'Tania said. Selena looked at her and nodded, gasping for air. Together they entered the hut with Milæyka right behind them.

"We have to continue our exploration," Caleb was saying. "Meet us by the ship in four days' time."

"It will take you that long?" Callix said with surprise.

"You never know. We have another day of walking through these plains and then we have to scale the mountain. It could take two to four days and I'm betting on four," Caleb responded.

"We'll accompany you to the edge of the plains,"

Calder said. "We can get you to the base of the mountain by nightfall, then find our way back here."

❈ ❈ ❈ ❈ ❈

It was agreed. The two boys accompanied the group to the foot of the mountain.

"Goodbye," Calder said.

"See you later," Callix said, with a wink to 'Tania, who blushed.

"Wait, Callix?" 'Tania called to him.

"Yeah, Elizabeth?"

"There's something you should know if you're coming back with us."

Callix cocked his head and gave her a questioning smile, "What?"

"My real name's 'Tania. My sisters and I are the royal princesses of Faerie." 'Tania gestured towards Caleb, "This is our adopted brother, Sir Caleb Læil."

'Tania smiled apologetically as Callix backed up into the grass, his face ashen. Then the sun went behind the mountain and darkness fell.

Chapter 17

_____Scaling_____

Lesson number one. Scaling a wall is stupid and should never be attempted unless one has no choice, Selena thought. The princesses and Caleb were resting on a ledge fifteen feet from the ground. Scaling those fifteen feet involved Selena falling twice, Caleb cutting his ankle about half an inch deep, and 'Tania flying up the mountain finding good handholds for the group.

"Why...do...we...have to scale the mountain?" Milæyka panted as she reached the ledge.

"No...choice." Caleb panted back.

'Tania was floating next to the ridge looking perfectly at peace. Selena felt a pang of jealousy.

"You know it's not really vertical," 'Tania said.

"Then what is it?" Demy asked.

"Well, it's a mountain, so you guys are really climbing at a slight incline because the top of the mountain is narrower than the base," 'Tania said with a shrug.

Selena rolled her eyes. *Of course it's an incline. It's just a really small one.* "How tall is this mountain?" she asked, mostly directing her question at Caleb.

145

"If we climb to the top, about four thousand feet," Caleb said. He was greeted by several gasps and moans.

"But...." he said in a teasing tone. "If we climb about one thousand feet, we can walk over the land bridge and find what we're looking for."

Selena smiled. Caleb was growing on her. He really wasn't that bad. The more time she spent with him, the less like a jerk he seemed and the more she realized he hadn't been acting a whole lot when he was Jake in the mortal world.

"So, what direction to the land bridge?" 'Tania asked.

"Up and over that way." Caleb pointed to the left.

Selena watched as 'Tania flew in the direction he pointed, scanning the terrain and surveying handholds. She disappeared around the side of the mountain momentarily then flew back down towards them.

"Okay... about five hundred feet up, the mountain is covered in little holes; some of them are glowing," 'Tania said and looked at Caleb.

"Dwarf mines. The glowing ones are furnaces. The rest are just air holes unless they use gnomes."

"Gnomes?" Selena asked, confused.

"If the dwarfs use gnomes to help them in the mines, we have to be careful that they don't bite our fingers when we put them in the holes."

Selena's eyes widened. "Good to know," she muttered as she put her hands on the wall to start climbing. Above her she could hear 'Tania shouting directions to the climber in front. Five hundred feet didn't seem like much—less than 200 meters—but when you're climbing up an almost vertical wall, it takes a while. *I can't take much more of this*, Selena thought.

She was in the middle; Caleb, Milæyka, and Demy were climbing in front of her; and Autumn, December, and Bella were climbing behind her. 'Tania was flying above Caleb telling him which way to go. *It's strange to watch 'Tania fly*, Selena thought. *She is just there. She just hovers there unmoved by wind or air.* Selena's hand missed the next handhold and she was jolted back to reality as her feet lost balance too. "Help!" she cried as she felt her other hand starting to slip.

✳ ✳ ✳ ✳ ✳

'Tania turned in midair as she heard Selena's cry for help and almost fell out of the air when she saw Selena dangling by one hand. She soared down and grabbed Selena's other hand, leading it to a handhold, and then doing the same with her feet. When Selena was on the wall again, 'Tania allowed herself to breathe.

"Be careful, Selena," she said.

Selena just nodded and began climbing again. "How much farther until the holes?"

"Not far. Caleb's there already." Just then they heard a shout of pain. 'Tania flew up and came to a hover beside Caleb.

"What's wrong?" she asked.

"Stupid gnome bit me!" Caleb said in indignation.

'Tania laughed softly. "Watch out everyone. The gnomes bite!" she yelled down the slope. She heard several moans and she laughed again. It was like being at school when everybody else but you was complaining about a project. 'Tania did a loop-the-loop and stopped by Milæyka.

"Don't put your hand there!" she yelled. But it was too late. Milæyka pulled her hand back quickly as the fire within the hole shot out, but it caught her hand.

"Ow!" Milæyka yelled, her other hand coming loose to support the burn.

"Milæyka!" 'Tania screamed as her sister started to

147

fall. 'Tania shot down and grabbed her sister's arms. "I can't hold you!" She yelled, concentrating all her energy towards keeping her and her sister aloft. Milæyka was still trying to soothe her hand. "December!" 'Tania shouted. "Make it rain! We need the water to soothe Milæyka's burn!"

'Tania felt an inner battle as she tried to stay airborne. She concentrated on her energy, bringing it up through her feet to her chest then flinging it out through her arms. She could feel the rain coming down on her back. Suddenly a siren went up and a scream.

"Intruder alert! Intruder alert!" Dwarves were swarming over the mountainside. 'Tania could see them trying to loosen her family's grip on the mountain. *What do I do?* She screamed in her head. *I can't save them all!* She could barely carry Milæyka, who was slipping. 'Tania made another surge of power and managed to gain a couple feet.

Then she felt a huge power rising in her feet. She concentrated on bringing it up to her chest, careful not to lose any power. It reached her heart and she flung it out to her arms. To her surprise Milæyka shot up like a cork. *I extended my power*, she thought. *If I touch somebody else they can fly too.* When she stopped concentrating on the power, Milæyka dropped again and nearly wrenched 'Tania's arm out of her socket. 'Tania quickly started concentrating again.

"Milæyka!" she yelled through gritted teeth, fighting to be heard over the rain and sirens. "Tell everybody to grab on and don't let go!" 'Tania concentrated on flying over all her siblings and Caleb, each time feeling a slight pressure as they each grabbed on. 'Tania could feel her strength failing. *I have to make it to the bridge*, she thought. She flew in a zigzag pattern, struggling to keep the power flowing through her body. *Almost there!* 'Tania could feel the power slipping away. *Made it.* 'Tania staggered to the ground, falling over almost immediately. Channeling so much power had weakened her considerably.

"I did it!" she murmured before falling asleep.

Chapter 18

____The Guardian____

The land bridge was nothing but a spit of land connecting the two mountains. Just looking at it made Selena weak at the knees. "We have to cross that?" she said a little too loudly. 'Tania shifted in her sleep.

"It has to be like a mile long," Demy said, looking at the bridge.

"Oh come on guys, it can't be worse than scaling the mountainside," Milæyka pointed out. Just then a rumble shook the mountain as a huge explosion from the dwarf mines caused rocks to come sliding down. Autumn and December yanked 'Tania out of the way before she could be crushed by a particularly big rock. "Okay, maybe this is worse than scaling the mountain," Milæyka amended sitting at the beginning of the spit.

"Is it just me, or does it get narrower at the center?" Demy asked.

"Well, it's like four feet here. It looks less than two feet there…" Selena said trailing off into a discouraging silence. The seven who were awake stared out over the bridge.

"Let's go one at a time," Caleb said.

"Should we wake 'Tania up? She's the only one who can save us just like she did when we were scaling the mountain," Milæyka was concerned. The journey was becoming more and more dangerous.

"No… Let her sleep. We'll take our chances. Demy, if you see the rocks beginning to fall, try to reinforce them with your powers. You'll go second to last. Wake 'Tania before you come over." Caleb took a deep breath and started walking over the bridge. It wasn't really that hard.

When Caleb was halfway across, he turned around and motioned for the next person to come across. Selena took a deep breath and started across the bridge. *Don't look down. Don't look down*, she repeated in her head as she got further and further along the bridge. She had been wrong. The middle of the bridge was less than a foot across and it stayed that way for a while.

She stared at Caleb, who had reached the other side. Selena saw him motion to the person behind her to follow. In front of her was the narrowest part of the bridge. It had spidery cracks in it from previous crossers. "Don't look down, don't look down." Selena turned her mental reminders into a chant as she stepped out over small spidery cracks. Selena took another step forward just as the rumbles began. They started gently, and then increased in magnitude. Selena leapt for the safer ground, hitting it just as more spidery cracks began to appear all throughout the bridge and the existing ones enlarged.

"Run!" Demy yelled. The last couple of princesses ran across the bridge as fast as they could without tripping and falling. When they reached the narrow part they had to leap.

"'Tania! Wake up!" Selena called across the chasm.

Demy was shaking her as hard as she could. 'Tania started awake and saw the bridge crumbling.

"Come on!" she yelled to Demy as she took to the air. Selena could tell from Demy's face that she was the reason the bridge was still intact. As soon she stopped concentrating, the bridge would finish collapsing.

"Oh dear."

Demy started running down the broken bits of bridge, 'Tania flying above her. 'Tania soared ahead and landed beside Selena. "You think she can make it?" she asked worriedly.

"I hope so. If she can't do you think you can save her?"

'Tania shook her head. "It took more effort than usual just to get myself across. I don't think I can do two people again." 'Tania looked worried. They both looked at Demy running across the bridge that was steadily falling apart despite her concentration.

"Jump!" Caleb yelled as Demy lost control of the rocks.

Demy made a leap and missed.

"Demy!" the sisters shouted, almost in unison. They ran to the edge and looked down.

"Thank goodness," Autumn said. Demy was there. She was about a foot down hanging on an exposed tree limb.

"Help me get her up," Caleb said, leaning down to grab her hands.

Together, the group managed to haul her up to the ledge.

"Thanks," she said, clutching at a small wound in her side.

"Onward?" asked Caleb.

"Onward," confirmed Selena.

The seven princesses stopped when they heard a loud

roar coming from a dark passage to their left.

"What was that?" Selena asked nervously.

"The guardian," Caleb said grimly.

"I hate it when he gets grim," 'Tania said as another roar came accompanied by several heavy footfalls. "That normally means something bad is coming."

* * * * *

"Quickly! Up there." Caleb was pointing to another dark hole about twenty feet above them. There was a ledge right outside the hole that they would be able to stand on. *I can't fly again*, 'Tania thought as she grabbed the wall with her hands. Carrying her family up the mountainside had taken its toll on 'Tania. She felt drained of energy, like when you've been playing a game that involves running too long and you're beyond tired. The footsteps were getting closer.

"Caleb, what's the guardian?" 'Tania asked.

"Uh... nothing to worry about... just a small little teensy... uh... dragon," Caleb said slowly and with great stalling pauses.

"*A What*?!" 'Tania yelled at him.

"The guardian's a dragon."

If I was a weak person I would be unconscious, 'Tania thought as the dragon roared again. 'Tania turned around and nearly fainted. The dragon was huge—at least twenty feet tall. It had red scales and purple spikes and horns. Its eyes sparkled every color. It was like looking into a prism. *It's a dragon. It's a dragon*, 'Tania said over and over again in her head as she climbed the wall. She knew she was hyperventilating. *Calm down. It's not going to hurt you.*

Bella screamed as a ribbon of flame shot right next to her head.

Okay, maybe it will hurt you. Just climb faster. 'Tania was at the end of the procession. Caleb, Selena, and Demy had already reached the ledge and were aiming their swords at the dragon's head when it got too close. The dragon reared up on its hind legs blew fire into the sky. 'Tania had to flatten herself against the wall to avoid being hit by the dragon's front feet. *Oh my gosh*, 'Tania cried in her head. She made another effort to climb faster.

"Come on 'Tania! You can do it," Selena called from the ledge. 'Tania used a brief flight instinct to make her body weigh less. She wasn't flying, but she wasn't being pulled by gravity either. The dragon whipped its tail around and 'Tania had to leap up to the ledge to avoid being hit. As soon as 'Tania touched the ledge, the dragon retreated back into the cave.

"That was exciting," 'Tania said, her eyes wide.

Caleb laughed once and then became serious again. "Only one thing left to do."

Selena nodded.

"The Ancient One."

Chapter 19

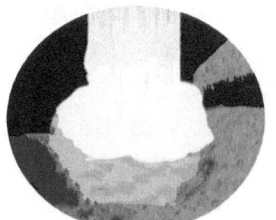

_____The Ancient One_____

"Hello younglings, welcome to Arcadia," said a deep voice inside the cave. "You have traversed the continent to find me, facing many challenges along the way, but avoiding those set up for you by those who gave you your questions."

The sisters shot each other puzzled looks. *Who is she talking about?* 'Tania wondered. *Our parents...* 'Tania's thoughts stuttered when she realized she had just acknowledged Thíshién as her father.

"As a reward for your bravery I shall answer your questions without asking for payment. I believe the efforts it took to get here is payment enough. I shall answer the questions you wish to know."

"Oh Ancient One," Caleb said getting to one knee. "We only wish to know what trouble awaits our kingdom."

"It is true you want to know that young Caleb, but you also wish me to tell you the answer to the question that disturbs your soul," said the voice slowly. 'Tania thought it sounded like a woman's voice. "Come inside so I can see you." Caleb walked in immediately.

"Should we go in?" Demy asked.

"I don't think Thíshién would send us to find her if she was dangerous," Selena said with a shrug.

"She can't be more dangerous than the dragon," 'Tania said, and followed Caleb in. "Whoa." The cavern was like a whole new world. *It's like all those books about worlds inside of worlds*, 'Tania thought. There was a rushing waterfall in the background running over a grass bridge, and lush green grass growing around a river. But the most amazing thing in the cavern was the creature sitting in the middle of the island located in the center of the wide river.

She looked like a dragon, but the energy she let off gave the sisters a safe feeling. Her scales were pale blue and her horns and spikes were an ever-changing rainbow. *Like Melody's eyes*, 'Tania thought. Then she looked into the Ancient One's eyes and all other thoughts drifted away. It was like looking into a crystal ball. There were images after images of 'Tania throughout her life. They started when she was little, running past every occasion that 'Tania remembered happening. Images of memories that were stuck in 'Tania's head, like her first day of kindergarten, her birthdays, and her first day of middle school. 'Tania paid rapt attention as she watched herself step into Faerie, followed by her training and scenes from the adventures she had had on the way here. Then she saw herself standing where she was. 'Tania gasped as images she had never seen before flicked by in rapid succession, only showing 'Tania, the people around her were a blur.

It's my future, 'Tania thought. *I look happy*. 'Tania watched as her wedding day passed by and then she thought she heard the voices of children laughing. The slideshow ended and 'Tania looked around at her siblings. They were each staring at the Ancient One with a similar look of awe. As 'Tania watched, one by one, her siblings shows ended and they each looked up.

"Thank you, younglings. It takes a great leap of faith to step into my cave and look into my eyes at the slideshow of your lives." The Ancient One looked down with upon the girls with a soft expression.

"Your Majesty," Caleb said bowing low. The princesses followed suit.

"No need to bow younglings, for you are royalty too. The last of the royal line. Great things are in store for you if you survive the coming battle. For the future I showed you is not set in stone, if you shall fail, no hope remains in our kingdom."

"Wait, you said *our* kingdom. Isn't our kingdom different from yours?"

Demy asked at the same time Bella asked, "I thought our win was prophesized. How can we lose?"

"The creatures like to think of our world as two kingdoms, the Island of Faerie, and the Island of Others, but what they don't see is that this is the World of Faeire on two different islands. We are all in one kingdom, and we will all be affected if you guys don't succeed."

"But—" Bella began again, but the Ancient One interrupted.

"If you try your hardest and are absolutely prepared, then you *will* defeat the evils that await you."

"So what you're saying is, don't get cocky." 'Tania summarized.

The Ancient One let out a small laugh. The laugh made 'Tania smile, it was so kind and gentle and at the same time it was deep and filling. It reverberated around the spacious cavern, echoing back towards the Ancient One.

"Now, the question you came here for, the question Caleb asked has a very simple answer. The evil that awaits you when you return, the monsters coming at the New Year, are from the Barred Lands."

159

"What are the Barred Lands?" Milæyka asked.

"The Barred Lands are home to the Failed Species. They are creatures that didn't turn out right, that were hidden from view. Creatures that have defects like limbs that bend the wrong way or have their brain in their feet. The Barred Lands lay beyond our borders, across a trench so deep nobody has figured out the exact depth, we only know it's deeper than our instruments can measure." Caleb explained, never taking his eyes off of the Ancient One.

"He is right, but monsters coming at the New Year are not the monster that is spoken of in the Prophecy. That monster has a feared name I refuse to utter in my cave. It will take each of you at your full power to defeat. It is by far the hardest challenge the kingdom faces."

The sisters looked at each other in alarm. *How can we defeat this monster if we can't even battle a giant chicken without getting hurt?* 'Tania thought, thinking of the Volacocary battle.

The Ancient One continued, "The monster in the prophecy is a monster who, like me, is first born in the land." The sisters exchanged a confused glance.

"I don't understand, I thought you were the firstborn. How can there be two firstborns?" 'Tania said.

"The monster is the first born of the Failed Species." Caleb's mouth opened in an O.

"So this big monster is the first born of the defective creatures, just like you were the first born of creatures here?" Selena asked.

"Indeed youngling. Just remember, believe in yourself, all of you. To be at your full powers, you have to let go of all the physics you learned on Earth and believe that anything can happen." The Ancient One looked at the siblings with a compassionate smile. "You can do it." She encouraged gently.

"Time is running out, we must move on. There is a

question you haven't asked that is bothering many of you, but one of you more than the others." The Ancient Once paused and smiled again.

"The marriage spell or curse—as you put it—can be broken. It will be broken. If true love is earned before the first kiss."

"I'm not sure what you mean," Selena asked. 'Tania had a strong suspicion that Selena had been the one who wanted the question answered.

"Because of the curse, love means nothing to Faeries," the Ancient One continued, her voice sounding oddly stiff all of a sudden, like this was a grudge she hadn't gotten over yet. "They think they know. They think 'I can only fall in love with the person who is right for me.'"

"But isn't that true?" Caleb asked, earning a disapproving glare from the Ancient One.

"No, Faeries choose to fall in love with the person with whom they connect. They take it for granted. What they don't know is that they can change fate of the curse. If true love is found *without* kissing, if a couple falls in love before they share their first kiss, then the spell will be broken."

The siblings lapsed into silence as that sunk in. It reminded 'Tania of all the movies she had seen in the Mortal world, where the hero has a crush on the girl and they have an adventure together, falling in love before they reach the final scene, where they kiss.

"Um... Mrs. Ancient One?" December asked timidly.

The Ancient One let out a soft laugh, "Yes, youngling?"

"You said, to be at our full powers.... does that mean we haven't reached them yet?"

"Indeed, none of you have reached the full extent of your powers. Some of you are close, some are afraid to test their limits. Some of you have areas of your power that you haven't even discovered yet. Only through yourself can you find how to discover these. It is easiest when you are experiencing a strong emotion because it runs through you like a current. Several of you know this. Some were close to the answer." The Ancient One paused and looked down at them.

"The last question you all are thinking is about my comment when you first heard my voice. The person who set a trap for you was the Dictator."

"I thought he was dead," Caleb said.

"No… The dictator is not a faerie and he has powers beyond most sorcerers. He left before your father could stab him. He set a trap for you. He knows that if you return, you can defeat the monsters. He doesn't want that. He wants to rule." The Ancient One stood up suddenly and went to a plant near the edge of the moat. "This plant here blooms a flower every time a spell is cast, and the flowers fall when the spell is undone. Because of the dictator, it is bursting with bloom." The Ancient One sighed again as she walked back to the group.

"Why didn't we fall in the trap?" Demy asked.

"You went to the Elvin Kingdom. If you had not, you would have been slaughtered as soon as you left the forest." The Ancient One let loose a small chuckle at the surprise and horror on the princesses' faces.

The Ancient One became serious again and addressed each of them personally.

"Caleb, you *are* the brother of the lost ones. Never forget that and never let it bother you." 'Tania watched as Caleb's eyes locked onto the Ancient One's eyes. *He must be seeing the future*, she thought.

"Selena, only through trusting others can you be truly happy." Selena looked down at her feet and then at Caleb before her eyes also locked onto the Ancient One's.

"Milæyka, don't be a stickler for what you know and what you want. Be flexible. Allow new traditions to fill your life and make you happy." Milæyka nodded. Deep in her heart, 'Tania knew that the Ancient One was referring to Talon, Milæyka's betrothed, when she had said that.

"Autumn, learn the ways of nature to help center yourself. Think of it like yoga." The Ancient One smiled.

"December, always remember that weather is a complicated tool. If you can learn to control it to the point of making it rain on one flower, you will be able to control all you want." December's eyes filled with longing as she heard the Ancient One's words. 'Tania too had a slight pang of jealousy at all the power December would have if she mastered the weather.

"Bella, don't be afraid to call animals and talk to them. Use your whistle to talk to mythological animals. You never know what useful tips they have." Bella fingered her necklace, its well-worn sides standing out against the blue of her clothes.

"Demy, you can do more than create monsters and hold things together. Turn your mind towards creating and play around with that. To a well-practiced hand, you may find you can create and destroy what nature takes years to produce... Your power is powerful, if that makes sense." Demy nodded.

"And 'Tania," the Ancient One paused, looking at 'Tania up and down. "Don't be afraid to discover yourself. It may help you more than you know." 'Tania looked into the Ancient One's eye and saw herself, not much older, surrounded by a bright white light.

"All of you, look to yourselves, and don't let greed infiltrate your minds." The Ancient One finished her speech and bowed her head. "The magic in here has messed with time. When you leave, it will have been four days since you left the Plains of Ramin. You will find the two lost ones waiting for you by the boat. The tunnel in the back will send you straight to your ship." The Ancient

163

One's kind eyes lingered over each of them a moment longer.

"Thank you, Ancient One. We will take your words to heart." Caleb gestured to the princesses to follow him as he walked to the chute.

"Do you think we can do it?" 'Tania asked her sisters as they watched Caleb disappear from view.

"Yes 'Tania. I think we can." Demy said with a distant expression.

"If we do what the Ancient One said, I think we'll kick butt," Milæyka said with a slight smile. Bella smiled too before sliding down into the chute.

"Do you think Dakar will come?" Demy asked, looking at the whistle he had given her.

"Of course he will. And when we get home you two can announce your engagement," December said with a small laugh sliding down the chute.

"Was she kidding?" Demy asked as she blushed.

"About Dakar coming? No. About your engagement? Probably." Demy rolled her eyes as she slid down the chute after December.

"You know, we could start a band here in Faerie." 'Tania said.

"What would we call it?" Milæyka asked as she sat down at the entrance to the chute.

"TSP. The Seven Princesses," 'Tania said with a smile.

"Good idea. We can put Caleb, Callix, Calder, Dakar, and Talon on the instruments." Milæyka smiled and pushed herself down the chute.

"It really is a good idea, 'Tania," Selena said. "Do you think we'll ever get home?"

'Tania was silent for a moment. "*This* is our home, Selena." Selena nodded and slid out of sight. *I am home*, 'Tania thought as she lowered herself into the chute. *Faerie is my home. Forever.* 'Tania took one last look at the

Ancient One, who was dozing peacefully, then slid down into darkness to a new journey, new friends, a new life, and a new home.

List of Characters

Girls

Milæyka
The first-born septuplet princess, Milæyka has the power to command people. She has a stone of truth that turns red when someone lies. Her symbol is a butterfly. Her colors are pink and yellow. Her horse's name is Persuasive Reason.

Selena
The second-born septuplet princess, Selena has the power to turn invisible and read minds. She has a telekinetic necklace. Her symbol is a coyote. Her colors are midnight blue and beige. She is dating Caleb. Her horse's name is Mind Reader.

Demeter
The third-born septuplet princess, Demy has the power to manipulate rock. She has a wishing leather that creates illusions. Her symbol is a dragon. Her colors are peach and sky blue. Her horse's name is Emerald Isle.

Titania
The fourth-born septuplet princess, 'Tania has the power to fly. She has a shield cloak to protect her from arrows and indirect sword blows, and blend her into the scenery. Her symbol is a unicorn. Her colors are royal blue and pale pink. Her horse's name is Skye and she has holographic wings.

December
The fifth-born septuplet princess, December has the power to manipulate the weather. She has a morphing jacket that can turn into clothing of any kind and number. Her symbol is an arctic hare. Her colors are forest green and peachy red. Her horse's name is Elemental Beauty.

Autumn
The sixth-born princess, Autumn has the power over nature. She has a split necklace that can create a gap in the earth of any size and width. Her symbol is a griffin. Her colors are Kelly green and light green. She likes Calder. Her horse's name is Season Coming.

Bella
The seventh-born septuplet princess, Bella has the power to talk to animals. She has a whistle that can call any mythological animal. Her symbol is a kitten. Her colors are periwinkle and light purple. Her horse's name is Animal Call.

Melody
The septuplet's adopted sister, Melody is a land-mermaid. Her eyes are faceted and both her fingernails and a streak in her hair change color with her mood. Her colors are blue and sea green. Her symbol is a dolphin. Her horse's name is Claro de Luna Armonia.

Emmaralda
The Queen of Faerie, biological mother to the septuplets. Her symbol is a moon. Her colors are white blue and electric blue.

Cassia
Dakar's sister and heir to the elvin throne. She has a gift of healing.

Lizzie
An elvin nurse and 'Tania's friend.
Queen Caia
The elvin queen.

Boys

Talon
A knight in the palace. His colors are dark grey and light grey. His symbol is an iron dragon.

Caleb
Thíshién's adopted son and therefore adopted brother of the princesses, Caleb is in love with Selena. His colors are red and black. His symbol is a werewolf. His horse's name is WereWolf. He has a compass of wisdom that points wherever he wants to go. He is a triplet, with his two brothers being Callix and Calder, who are not adopted by Thíshién.

Dakar
An elvin prince. His sister is Cassia. His colors are dark green and lime green. His symbol is a stag. He is 863 years old.

Callix
Callix was raised with Calder in the Plains of Ramin after being kidnapped at age seven. His colors are maroon and light blue. His symbol is an eagle. His horse's name is Aquila Colpo. He has a crush on 'Tania.

Calder

He was raised in the Plains of Ramin with Callix after being kidnapped at two and a half. His colors are rust red and green. His symbol is a seal.

Thíshién

King of faerie. Biological father to the septuplets. His colors are red and yellow-orange.

King Damir

Elvin king.

Sir Kaill

Sword master, Thíshién's second in command.

Dictator

Evil being intent on destroying Faerie.

Titus

Thíshién's brother. Original adoptive father of Caleb. Disappeared in battle seventeen years ago.

Creatures

Elves

Have wings, live on Island of Others.

Faeries

Live on the island of Faerie. Un-winged. Live about 500 years.

Ancient One

The first-born creature in Faerie. Full of knowledge.